How To Cook Husbands

by Elizabeth Strong Worthington

Author of "The Little Brown Dog"

"The Biddy Club"

"They are really delicious

—when properly treated."

Originally published in 1898.

Dedication

To a dear little girl who will some

day, I hope, be skilled in all branches

of matrimonial cookery.

I

A while ago I came across a newspaper clipping—a recipe written by a Baltimore lady—that had long lain dormant in my desk. It ran as follows:

"A great many husbands are spoiled by mismanagement. Some women go about it as if their husbands were bladders, and blow them up; others keep them constantly in hot water; others let them freeze, by their carelessness and indifference. Some keep them in a stew, by irritating ways and words; others roast them; some keep them in pickle all their lives. Now it is not to be supposed that any husband will be good, managed in this way—turnips wouldn't; onions wouldn't; cabbage-heads wouldn't, and husbands won't; but they are really delicious when properly treated.

"In selecting your husband you should not be guided by the silvery appearance, as in buying mackerel, or by the golden tint, as if you wanted salmon. Be sure to select him yourself, as taste differs. And by the way, don't go to market for him, as the best are always brought to your door.

"It is far better to have none, unless you patiently learn to cook him. A preserving kettle of the finest porcelain is the best, but if you have nothing but an earthenware pipkin, it will do, with care.

"See that the linen, in which you wrap him, is nicely washed and mended, with the required amount of buttons and strings, nicely sewed on. Tie him in the kettle with a strong cord called Comfort, as the one called Duty is apt to be weak. They sometimes fly out of the kettle, and become

burned and crusty on the edges, since, like crabs and oysters, you have to cook them alive.

"Make a clear, strong, steady fire out of Love, Neatness, and Cheerfulness. Set him as near this as seems to agree with him. If he sputters and fizzles, don't be anxious; some husbands do this till they are quite done. Add a little sugar, in the form of what confectioners call Kisses, but no vinegar or pepper on any account. A little spice improves them, but it must be used with judgment.

"Don't stick any sharp instrument into him, to see if he is becoming tender. Stir him gently; watching the while lest he should lie too close to the kettle, and so become inert and useless.

"You cannot fail to know when he is done. If thus treated, you will find him very digestible, agreeing nicely with you and the children."

"So they are better cooked," I said to myself, "that is why we hear of such numbers of cases of marital indigestion—the husbands are served raw—fresh—unprepared."

"They are really delicious when properly treated,"—I wonder if that is so.

But I must pause here to tell you a bit about myself. I am not an old maid, but, at the time this occurs, I am unmarried, and I am thirty-four years old—not quite beyond the pale of hope. Men and women never do pass beyond that—not those of sanguine temperament at any rate. I am neither rich nor poor, but repose in a comfortable stratum betwixt and between. I keep house, or rather it keeps me, and a respectable woman who, with her husband, manages my domestic affairs, lends the odor of sanctity and propriety to my single existence. I am of medium height, between blond and brunette, and am said to have a modicum of both brains and good looks.

The recipe I read set me a-thinking. I was in my library, before a big log fire. The room was comfortable; glowing with rich, warm firelight at that moment, but it was lonesome, and I was lonely.

Supposing, I said to myself, I really had a husband; how should I cook him?

The words of an old lady came into my mind. She had listened to this particular recipe, and after a moment's silence had leaned over, and whispered in my ear:

"First catch your fish."

But supposing he were now caught, and seated in that rocker across from me, before this blazing fire.

I walked to the window—to one side of me lives a little thrush, at least she is trim and comely, and always dresses in brown. Just now she is without her door, stooping over her baby, who is sitting like a tiny queen in her chariot, just returned from an airing.

It isn't the question of husband alone—he might be managed—roasted, stewed, or parboiled, but it's the whole family—a household. Take the children, for instance; if they could be set up on shelves in glass cases, as fast as they came, all might be well, but they will run around, and Heaven only knows what they will run into. Why, had I children, I should plug both ears with cotton, for fear I should hear the door-bell. I know it would ring constantly, and such messages as these would be hurled in:

"Several of them have been arrested for blowing up the neighbors with dynamite firecrackers."

"Half a dozen of them have tumbled from off the roof of the house. They escaped injury, but have thrown a nervous lady, over the way, into spasms."

"One or two of them have just been dragged from beneath the electric cars. They seem to be as well as ever, but three of the passengers died of fright."

Just think of that! What should I do?

Keep an extra maid to answer the bell, I suppose, and two or three thousand dollars by me continually, to pay damages.

What a time poor Job had of it answering his door bell, and how very unpleasant it must have been to receive so many pieces of news of that sort, in one morning!

Clearly I am better off in my childless condition, and yet—
—

Little Mrs. Thrush is just kissing her soft, round-faced cherub. I wish she would do that out of sight.

Now as to husbands again, if I had one, what should I do with him?

I might say, Sit down.

Supposing he wouldn't. What then?

Cudgels are out of date. Were he an alderman, I might take a Woman's Club to him, but a husband has been known to laugh this instrument to scorn.

But supposing he sat down. What then? He might be a gentleman of irascible, nasty temper, and in walking about my room, I might step on his feet. These irritable folk have such large feet, at least they are always in the way, and always being stepped on no matter how careful one tries to be.

What then?

I decline to contemplate the scene.

Plainly I am better off single.

I walk to my front window, and stretch my arms above my head. There is a light fall of snow upon the ground. This late snow is trying: in its season, it is beautiful; but out of season, it breeds a cheerlessness that emphasises one's loneliness. I look out through the leafless trees toward the lake, but it is hidden by the whirling, eddying snowflakes. I see Mr. Thrush hurrying home to his little nest.

"Yes," I say to myself, repeating my last thought with a certain obstinacy, "yes, I am better off without a husband, and yet I wish I had one—one would answer, on a pinch— one at a time, at least. A husband is like a world in that respect; one at a time, is the proper proportion."

"It's far better to have none, unless you learn to cook him."
These words recurred to me, just as I was on the point of
taking a life partner, in a figurative sense.

The woman that deliberates is lost; consequently, as it
won't do to think the matter over, I plunge in.

My spouse is now pacing up and down the room in a
rampant manner, complaining of his dinner, the world in
general, and me in particular.

What am I to do?

Charles Reade has written a recipe that applies very well
just here. It is briefly expressed:

"Put yourself in his place."

I could not have done this a few years ago, but now I can.
Never, until I undertook the management of my business
affairs—never until I had some knowledge of business
cares and anxieties, the weight of notes falling due; the
charge of business honor to keep; the excited hope of
fortunate prospects; and the depression following hard
upon failure and disappointment—never until I learned all
this, did I realize what home should mean to a man, and
how far wide of the mark many women shoot, when they
aim to establish a restful retreat for their husbands.

I have returned to my domicile, after a fatiguing day up
town, with a feeling of exhaustion that lies far deeper than
the mere physical structure—a spent feeling as if I have
given my all, and must be replenished before I can make
another move. I once had a housekeeper whose very face I
dreaded at such times. She always took advantage of my

silence and my limp condition, to relate the day's disasters.
She had no knowledge of what a good dinner meant, and no
tact in falling in with my tastes or needs. On the contrary; if
there was a dish I disliked, it was sure to appear on those
most weary evenings. In brief, from the very moment I
reached home, she did nothing but brush my fur up, instead
of down, and I did nothing but spit at her.

Now, many women are like this housekeeper. I wonder
their husbands don't slay them. If you would look out in
my back yard, I fear you would see the bones of several of
these tactless, exasperating housekeepers, bleaching in the
wind and rain.

I marvel that other back yards are not filled with the bones
of stupid, tactless, irritating wives. The fact that no such
horror has as yet been unearthed, bears eloquent testimony
to the noble self-control and patience of many of the sterner
sex.

"Oh, that sounds well," said my neighbor, over the way,
"but then you forget we women have our trials too."

"Is it going to diminish those trials to make a raging lion
out of your husband?"

"No, but he ought to understand that we are tired, and that
our work is hard."

"Certainly," I said, "by all means; and by the time he
thoroughly understands, you generally have occasion to be
still more tired."

"Well, what would you do?"

"I'll tell you what I'd do; follow the advice of a sensible little friend of mine, who has four children all of an age, and has incompetent service to rely on, when she has any at all."

"And what is that, pray?"

"She says that come rain, hail, or fiery vapor, she takes a nap every day."

"I don't know how she manages it; I can't, and I have one less child than she, and a fairly good maid."

"Her children are trained, as children should be; the three younger ones take long naps after luncheon, and while they are sleeping, she gives the oldest child some picture book to look at, and simple stories to read, and she herself goes to sleep in the same room with him. The little fellow keeps as still as a mouse."

"I think that is a cruel shame."

"So do I. It would be far kinder if she let him have his liberty, and stayed up to take care of him, and then became so tired out that, by the time her husband came home she would be unable to keep her mouth (closed for it is only a well rested woman who can maintain a cheerful silence), and avoid a family quarrel."

"No, I think it's better not to quarrel, but I can't take a nap, and often I'm so tired when Fred comes home, that, if he happens to be tired too, it's just like putting fire to gunpowder."

I knew that, for I had heard the explosions from across the street. You know in our climate, in the summer, people practically live in the street, with every window and door open; your neighbor has full possession of all remarks above E. And most of Mr. and Mrs. Purblind's notes on the tired nights, are above E.

I have no patience with that woman, anyhow. She hasn't the first idea of comfort and good cheer. Her rooms are always in disorder, and there is no suggestion of harmony in the furniture (on the contrary every article seems, as the French say, to be swearing at every other article); all her lights are high—why, I've run in there of an evening and found that man wandering around like an uneasy ghost, trying to find some easy spot in which he could sit down, and read his paper comfortably. He didn't know what was the matter—the poor wretches don't, but he was like a cat on an unswept hearth.

In contrast to this woman's stupidity, I have the natural loveliness of the little brown thrush, on my one side, and the hoary-headed wisdom of Mrs. Owl, on my other side.

Look at the latter a moment. Not worth looking at, you say; angular, without beauty of form or feature. Nothing but the humorous curve to her lips, and the twinkle in her eye, to attract one; nothing, unless it were a general air of neatness, intelligence, and good humor.

But I assure you that woman's worth living with if she is not worth looking at!

Now her spouse is one of those lowering fellows, the kind that seems to be at outs with mankind. Just the material to become sulky in any but the most skillful hands, the sort to degenerate into a positive brute, in such blundering hands as Mrs. Purblind's over the way.

I had a chance to watch this man one evening last summer. Having no domestic affairs of my own, as a matter of course I feel myself entitled to share my neighbors'. And this particular evening I was lonely. It was a nasty night, the fog blown in from the lake slapped one rudely in the face every time one looked out, and the air was as raw as a new wound—it went clear to the bone.

Now on such a night as this I have known Mrs. Purblind to serve her lord cold veal and lettuce, simple because it was July, and a suitable time for heat. And I assure you that sufficient heat was generated before this cold supper was consumed. But to return to Mrs. Owl, on that particular night. I saw her watching at door and window, for her partner was late. I peeped into the parlor, and it was as cosy and inviting as a glowing fire, a shaded lamp, and a comfortable sofa wheeled near the table, could make it.

By and by, he came glowering along. What will she say, I asked myself. Will it be:

"Oh, how late you are! What's the matter? What kept you? Well, come in, you must be cold. Lie down on the sofa while I get supper, but don't put your feet up till I get a paper for them to rest on."

All this would have answered well enough with a decent sort of a man, but this homo required peculiar treatment.

It was what she didn't say that was most remarkable.

After a cheerful "How-de-do" she didn't speak a word for some time, but walked into the house humming a lively air, and busied herself with his supper. She didn't set this in the dining room, but right before that open fire. Without any fuss or commotion she broiled a piece of steak over those glowing coals, while over her big lamp she made a cup of coffee, and in her chafing dish prepared some creamed potatoes. She had bread and butter ready, and some little dessert, and so with a wave of a fairy wand, as it seemed, there was the cosiest, most tempting little supper you ever saw on the table at his side.

Meanwhile he had found the sofa, the fire, and the lamp, and was reading his paper. He threw the latter down when supper was announced, and she joined him at the table; poured his coffee, ate a bit now and then for company, and talked—why, how that woman did talk! I couldn't hear a word that she said, but I knew by the expression of her face it was humorous; and laugh, how she laughed! and erelong he joined in—why, once he leaned back, and actually ha-haed.

When supper was over, she left him to his paper again, while she cleared everything away. Later on she joined him, and the next I knew they were playing chess, and still later, talking and reading aloud.

This is but a sample of her life with him—in everything she consults his mood, his comfort, his tastes. She never jars him—never rubs him the wrong way, and meanwhile she has all she wants, for she can do anything with him, and he thinks the sun rises and sets with her.

It is a good cook that makes an appetizing dish out of poor material, and when a woman makes a delicious husband out of little or nothing she may rank as a chef.

II

You may say all I have been describing belongs more properly to little Mrs. Thrush, on my right. Bless you! that woman doesn't have to think and plan to make things comfortable. Were she set down in the desert of Sahara, she would sweep it up, spread a rug; hang a few draperies, and lo! it would be cosy and home-like. She can't help being and doing just right, wherever she is put, and her husband is just like her, as good as gold. Why, that man would bore a woman of ingenuity—a woman who had a genius for contriving and managing. He doesn't need any cooking; he's ready to serve just as he is, couldn't be improved. There's absolutely nothing to be done. Mrs. Owl would get a divorce from him inside of a month, on the ground of insipidity. Her fine capabilities for making much out of nothing, would turn saffron for lack of use. Mr. Owl is the mate for her. To every man according to his taste; to every woman according to her need.

I am lying in the hammock, under the soft maple tree in my side yard, speculating on all these matters. Summer is now upon us, for we are in the midst of June. Yesterday was one of Lowell's rare days, but this morning the thermometer took offense, and rose in fury. I can see the quivering air as it radiates from the dusty, sun-beaten road, and a certain drowsy hum in the atmosphere, palpable only to the trained ear, tells of the great heat. Some of my neighbors are sitting on their galleries, reading or sewing; some, like myself, are lolling in hammocks; even the voices of the children have a certain monotonous tone, in harmony with the stupid heaviness of the day. Only the birds and squirrels show any life or spirit; the former are twittering above my head, courting, it may be, or possibly discussing some detail of household economy. They hop from bough to bough, touch up their plumage, and chirp in a cheerful, happy sort of fashion, as if this was their especial weather, as indeed it is. Up yonder tree, a squirrel is racing about, in the exuberance of his glee. He has done up his work, no doubt, and now is off for a frolic. I lie here, not a stone's throw from him, watching his merry antics, and rejoicing to think how free from fear he is, when all at once the leaves of his tree are cut by a flying missile, and the next second I see my gay fellow tumble headlong from the bough, and fall in a helpless little heap on the grass. I start up in affright, and hear a passing boy call out to another, over the way,

"I brought him down, Jim."

Involuntarily I clinch my hands.

"You little coward!" I exclaim, "it is you who should be brought down! You are too mean to live."

He laughs brutally, and goes on, whistling indifferently, while I pick up the dead squirrel lying at my feet.

I find myself crying, before I know it. Not alone with pity for the squirrel; something else is hurting me.

"Is this the masculine nature?" I ask some one—I don't know whom.

Perhaps it is one of those questions which are flung upward, in a blind kind of way, and which God sometimes catches and answers.

"Are they made this way? Was it meant that they should be brutal?"

I am still holding the squirrel and thinking, when I hear my name, and turning see my neighbor over the way, Mrs. Purblind's brother, standing near me.

"Good morning, Mr. Chance," I say, rather coldly.

All men are hateful to me at that moment; to my mind they all have that boy's nature, though they keep it under cover until they know you well, or have you in their power.

"The little fellow is dead, I suppose," he said.

"Yes," I answer with a sob which I turn away to conceal. I don't wish to excite his mirth. Of course he would only see something laughable in my grief, and he couldn't dream what I am thinking about.

"You mustn't be too hard on the boy, Miss Leigh," he says quietly; "it was a brutal act, but that same aggressiveness will one day give him power to battle in life against difficulties and temptations as well. It will make him able to protect those whom a kind Providence may put in his charge. Just now he doesn't know what to do with the force, and evidently has not had good teaching. I'm sorry he did this; it hurts me to see an innocent creature harmed, and still more I am sorry because it has hurt you."

He is standing near me now, and as I raise my eyes, I find him looking at me with a sweet earnestness, that wins me not only to forgive him for being a man, but to feel that perhaps men are noble, after all.

His look and tone linger with me long after he has gone, as a cadence of music may vibrate through the soul when both musician and instrument are mute.

The day after this of which I have been telling, I went to a picnic gotten up by Mrs. Purblind, for the entertainment and delectation of Mr. Purblind's cousin, now visiting her, a frivolous young thing, between whom and myself there was not even the weather in common, for she would label "simply horrid" a lovely gray day, containing all sorts of possibilities for the imagination behind its mists and clouds.

I didn't care for this picnic, and didn't see why I was invited as most of the guests were younger than myself. But it was one of those cases where a refusal might be misconstrued, and so I went. We sat around the white tablecloth en masse, for dinner; and in the course of the passing of viands, Miss Sprig was asked to help herself to olives that happened to be near her.

"Yes, do, while you have opportunity," said Mrs. Purblind.

"I always embrace opportunity," replied Miss Sprig with a simper. Whereat Mr. Chance, sitting next her, suggested that, as a synonym of opportunity, possibly he might stand in its stead.

I detest such speeches, they are properly termed soft, for
they certainly are mushy—lacking in stamina—fiber of any
sort. But I could have endured it, as I had endured much
else of the same sort that day, had it not come from Mr.
Chance. It may be foolish of me, but his tone and his words
of the day before were still with me. They were so
dignified, so sensible, so manly, that I respected and
admired him. Up to that time I had not felt that I knew him,
but after he spoke in that way, it seemed as if we were
acquainted. Now I saw how utterly mistaken I had been,
and I was mortified and disgusted.

The silly little speech I have quoted was not all, by any
means; there were more of the same kind, and actions that
corresponded. Evidently he was one of those instruments
which are played upon at will by the passing zephyr. With a
self-respecting woman, he was manly; with a vapid, bold
girl, he was silly and familiar. I decided that I liked
something more stable, something that could be depended
upon.

I was placed in a difficult position just then. Had I acted
upon my impulse, I should have risen and walked off—
such conduct is an affront to womanhood, I think; but I was
held in my place by a fear—foolish, yet grounded, that my
action would be regarded as an expression of jealousy, the
jealousy of an old maid, of a woman much younger and
prettier than herself. This is but one of the many instances
of the injustice of the world. I don't think that I am
addicted to jealousy, but I may not know myself. Possibly I
might have felt jealous had I been eclipsed by a beautiful or
gifted woman, but it would be impossible for me to
experience any such emotion on seeing a man with whom I
have but a slight acquaintance, devote himself to a girl
whom I should regard as not only my mental inferior, but

also as beneath me morally and socially as well. The only sensation of which I was cognizant was a disgust toward the man, and mortification over the mistaken estimate of his character, that had led me, the day before, to suppose him on a footing with myself.

As soon as possible after dinner I slipped away for a stroll. The place was very lovely, and I felt that if I could creep off with Mother Nature, she would smooth some cross-grained, fretful wrinkles that were gathering in my mind, and were saddening my soul. So when the folly and jesting were at their height I dipped into the thicket near at hand, and dodging here and there, jumping fallen logs, and untangling my way among the vines which embraced the stern old woods like seductive sirens, I at last struck a shaded path, which erelong led me down through a ravine to the waters of the big old lake. It too had dined, but instead of yielding itself to folly, was taking its siesta. Across its tranquil bosom the zephyrs played, stirring ripples and tiny eddies, as dreams may stir lights and shadows on the sleeping face.

I had not walked along the beach, with the waves sighing at my feet, and whispering all sorts of soothing nothings, for a great distance, before I began to experience that uncomfortable reaction which sometimes arises from splitting in two, as it were, standing off at a distance and looking oneself in the face. I realized that I had been something of a prig and considerable of a Pharisee. My late discomfort was not caused by the fact that a young girl had cheapened herself, but by the fact that a man had demeaned himself and in a manner involved me, inasmuch as I had been led the day before by a false estimate of his character to regard him as my social equal. After all it was this last that hurt most; it was my little self and not my brother about whom I was chiefly concerned.

I am not naturally sentimental or morbid, so I merely decided that internally I had made a goose of myself and not shown any surplus of nobility; and with a little sigh of satisfaction that I had given the small world about me no sign of my folly, I dismissed the subject and betook myself to an eager enjoyment of the day.

The soft June breeze played with my hair and gently and affectionately touched my face; the lake quivering and rippling with passing emotions stretched away from me toward that other shore which it kept secreted somewhere on its farther side. The very sight of it, with its shimmering greens, turquoise blue, and tawny yellow, cooled and soothed me, and ere I knew it, I had slipped into a pleasant, active speculation on matters of larger interest than the petty subjects which had lined my brow a moment before. I was walking directly toward one of my families, and it occurred to me that I might run in and make a call, while I was near at hand. I had first become interested in them at church. I was impressed by their cleanliness and regularity of attendance, and by a certain judicious arrangement of their children—the parents always sitting so as to separate the latter by their authority and order.

Another point that claimed my attention was that the children were changed each Sunday—a fresh three succeeding the first bunch, and on the third Sunday, one of the first three being added to a fresh two, to make up the proper complement. Both parents had a self-respecting, self-sacrificing look, as of people who had learned to help themselves cautiously from the family dish, and to "put their knives to their throats" before time; but kept all this to themselves, asking nothing from anyone, and making their little answer without murmur or complaint. I had, for some time, realized that the child who was now getting more than his share of sermons, by reappearing on the third Sunday, would soon be reduced to the level of his brethren, and a new relative would take the place which he had been filling as a matter of accommodation. I sought occasion to make the acquaintance of the mother of this fine brood, on the pretext of some church work, and after that became a regular visitor at their little home. The perfect equality of the parents; the deference with which they treated one another; and their quiet happiness, in spite of all labor and privation, made me realize that they might well extend a pitying thought to some of the apparently wealthy members of the church. We may yet live to see the day when a new scale shall come in vogue, and some Cr[oe]sus who now stands in an enviable light, shall then pass into his true position, and become an object of pity. Mere dollars and cents are a misleading criterion of poverty and wealth.

I had seen my friends, and found that the mother and her new nestling were in comparative comfort, and I was on the homeward stretch along the beach, when I saw Mr. Chance walking toward me.

"I was commissioned to look you up," he said.

"Thank you," I replied, "I have been of age for some years."

Of course he noticed the coolness in my voice, and in some way I divined that he knew the cause.

We went aboard our homeward-bound train about 5 o'clock.

Mr. Chance helped me on, and evidently expected to sit with me, but I thwarted him by dropping down beside an elderly lady, an acquaintance who happened to be in that coach. I felt no grudge against him, but I didn't care to have him pass from such a girl as Miss Sprig to me; his conduct with her impaired his value somewhat in my eyes. My elderly friend saw and recognized the situation, I am sure, and governed her later remarks accordingly.

Mr. Chance passed on, and took a seat with one of the superfluous men, for contrary to the rule on most such occasions, the male gender was in excess of the female. I had not expected him to return to Miss Sprig; men always become satiated with such girls, soon or late.

My elderly acquaintance entered upon an animated conversation, that became more and more personal, and finally reached a climax when she leaned over, and said in a semi-whisper:

"My dear Miss Leigh, you ought to marry."

I had been told this a number of times; any one would suppose, to listen to some of these women, that I had but to put out my hand, and pluck a man from the nearest bush.

"I don't doubt you will marry some day, but I'm afraid you may not choose wisely"—here she lowered her voice again—"after a man reaches thirty-five he becomes very fixed in his ways, and I don't think it's safe for a maiden lady to try to manage him; it needs some one of more experience."

I knew she had Mr. Chance in mind, and I was so indignant at being warned against a man who had never shown the first symptom of any such folly as addressing me, that the blood mounted to my hair.

Observing this, my elderly companion whispered:

"I wasn't thinking of any one, in particular, my dear;" upon which I grew more enraged, and the color in my face deepened until I must have resembled an irate old turkey gobbler—"not of any one in particular, my dear; but on general principles, I shouldn't advise such a match. A widower would be just the thing for you, and there always are widowers, and every year the list grows—death makes inroads, you know."

This idea, this hope of a second crop, as I had passed beyond the first picking, was comforting. I knew perfectly well whom she had in mind for me—a nice fat little widower, about fifty years old, who had been held on the marital spit, until he was done to a turn.

III

The summer was ended, and I was not married. I am speaking now from the standpoint of my neighbors; to my mind life did not swing on this hinge. I had my occupations—there were a goodly number of needy folk to be looked after; there was my reading; my music; my friends, and other pleasures, and altogether I felt I was very well off. Not that I was cynically opposed to marriage; I intended to marry, if the right man called, but if he did not I was content to end life as I had begun it—in single blessedness.

My neighbors, however, were of another mind—I must marry; and they kept making efforts to find some one who would fit, trying on one man after another, without his consent or mine, something as one would attempt to force clothes on a savage.

But in spite of all such friendly offices the summer was ended, and I was not married. I was thinking of it on this particular day, as I stood gazing from the window— thinking of it with a sort of quiet wonder, for with an entire neighborhood intent upon this end, it was rather surprising that I was not double by this time. Had they succeeded I should now occupy a very different attitude. It is only old bachelors and old maids who speculate and theorize on marriage; when people are really about it, they say little, and (it would often appear) think less.

It was a day for speculation—this particular one; the dead leaves were scurrying up the street as people ran for a train; a gusty wind was carrying all before it for the time being, like an overbearing debater. The trees shook and groaned, recoiled and shuddered, like human creatures in the blast; in their agitation dropping hosts of leaves that immediately slipped under covert, or else joined their fellows in the race up town. The sky was non-committal, and the lake looked dark and secretive, as if it meditated wreck and disaster.

It was only the middle of September, but there had been several of these days—a hint, perchance, of what was to come by and by, as a gay waltz strain sometimes dips into real life, and makes one look inward for a moment.

The house did not invite me just at this time, and the elements did; at least I felt that rising within me which tempted me forth to have a bout with them.

I was walking at a goodly pace along the Boulevard—for I love the lake in all its moods—when two men with anxious faces overtook, and hurried past me.

"There's been a wreck, miss," one of them—a man I knew—called back.

I quickened my pace, trying to peer through the sullen fog, as I ran. The occasional dull boom of a gun called "Help," from out the grayness, with pathetic persistency. Soon another sound caught my ear, or rather vibrated through my frame, for the ground beneath me seemed to tremble, and I turned to see the swift oncoming of the life-saving crew from a station below us.

I had barely time to jump one side, before the huge wagon, bearing the boat and its men, swept past me, every one of those splendid horses with his head lowered, and his fine muscles set for the race.

It was all done with the celerity and ease with which things are accomplished in dreams. The sudden halting of the big wagon; the swinging of the boat to the ground; the swift donning of the yellow oilskin suits by the crew; the launch, and before one had time to wink, the strong strokes in perfect time, that bore the boat up and down, and up again, on those tumultuous waves.

There were other spectators beside myself, standing with strained sight and hearing, and throbbing hearts, upon the strip of beach. And there were other workers beside the crew. I had thought we were a small community out there in the little suburb, and I gazed with wonder that morning at the crowd which seemed to have dropped from the sky, or come up from below.

The men were chiefly from the middle and laboring classes, for the others go in on early trains, but Randolph Chance was there, his newspaper work giving him his mornings. We spoke to one another, but entered into no conversation. My thought was with the doomed ship, and so was his.

"Will any of you boys join me in taking off some of those people?" he asked the men at hand.

"It's a rough sea, Mr. Chance."

"I know it, but I understand boating; I guess we can manage it."

"Don't you think the life-saving crew can do the work?" I asked.

"No," he answered shortly, "there won't be time for them to make enough trips. Come, boys, here she goes! Jump in, a half dozen of you that can pull oars."

There were boats enough, and soon there were men enough, for the human heart is kind and brave, and under a good leader men will walk up to Death himself without flinching.

Randolph Chance was big and strong, alert, and self controlled—a good leader. I realized all this just now, as I had not before, and I thought how strange it was that so much goodness should be bound up with so much folly. It was the old story of the wheat and the tares; and I said: "An enemy hath done this," and then I thought of Miss Sprig.

I don't like to dwell on that morning; the experience was new to me, and I can't forget it; I can't rid myself of the sound of those shrieks when the ship went down. She struggled like a human creature under a sudden blow— rocked, tottered, quivered, and then collapsed.

The little boats made five trips and brought ashore almost all the passengers and crew—all but one woman, and a little child.

I was one of the many who received the chilled and frightened victims of the storm, and indeed, as soon as we were able to dispose of the more delicate and needy ones, we turned our thought to the brave crews of the little boats, for their exertions had been almost superhuman, and they were well-nigh exhausted.

I bent over Randolph Chance, and begged him to take a little brandy some one had brought.

"Give it to the women," he said feebly.

"They are all cared for; I'm going to look out for you now, Mr. Chance."

"I wouldn't feel so done up," he said, "if it weren't for that woman. She begged me to save her, and she had a little child in her arms," and his voice broke.

"You mustn't think of her," I said, "you did all you could."

"Yes, I did my best to reach her, but before I could get there, she went down. I can never forget her face. Oh, at such a time a fellow can't help wishing he were just a little quicker, and just a little stronger."

He had risen from the beach where he had flung himself or fallen, on leaving the boat, but he fell again. I could plainly see that the exhaustion from which he suffered was due as much to mental distress as to physical effort, and I thought no less of him for that.

He was finally prevailed upon to get into the wagon which had brought the life-saving crew, and which was now loaded down with the other boatmen, and many of the passengers from the wreck, and so he was taken home. And I walked back alone, with a queer little feeling somewhere in the region of my heart.

Man, after all, is a harp, I said to myself; a good player— the right woman can draw forth wonderful music, but the wrong woman will call out nothing but discords.

Materials don't count for everything; there's a deal in the cooking.

I was on my way home, when I met two of my neighbors hurrying toward the scene—Mr. and Mrs. Daemon.

"You're too late," I said, "it's all over."

"I only heard of it a little while ago;" said Mrs. Daemon; "I was in the city, and I met Mr. Daemon who had just been told there was a wreck off this shore, and was coming out to see it, so we both took the first train."

They hurried on, wishing to see what they could, and I walked homeward.

Their appearance had slipped into my reflections as neatly as a good illustration slips into a discourse. I must tell you their story, and then see if you dare say man is not a harp, and woman not a harpist.

Years ago, when I was a child, I used to see my mother wax indignant over the wrongs inflicted upon one of her neighbors—a gentle little woman whose backbone evidently needed restarching. She was the mother of three children, and should have been a most happy wife, for her tastes were domestic—her devotion to her family unbounded. Unhappily, she was wedded to a man of overbearing, tyrannical temper—one of those ugly natures in which meanness is generated by devotion. The more he realized his power over his poor little wife, the more he bullied her, and beneath this treatment she faded, day by day, until finally she closed her tired, pathetic eyes forever. My mother used to say she had no doubt the man was overwhelmed by her death, and would have suffered from remorse, but for the injudicious zeal of some of the neighbors, who were so wrought up by this culmination of years of injustice and cruelty, that they attacked him fore and aft, as it were, creating a scandalous scene over the little woman's remains, accusing him of being her murderer, and assigning him to the warmest quarters in the nether world. As a result of this outbreak of public opinion the man hardened, and assumed a defiant attitude which he continued to maintain toward the neighbors for some years. In the midst of all this furor, the sister of the departed wife walked calm and still. The power of the silent woman has often been dwelt upon, but I really do not think that half enough has been said, although I am aware of committing an absurdity when I recommend voluble speech on the subject of silence. Jesting and paradoxes aside, however, the silent woman wields a power known only to the man toward whom her silence is directed.

In this particular case the power was all for the best. Erelong the sister-in-law obtained such mastery over the forlorn household that she held not only the fate of the little ones, but that of the father as well, in the hollow of her hand.

Two years slipped by, and then the neighborhood that had dozed off, as it were, awoke to hear that the sister was going to marry that awful man.

At once the vigilance committee arose, and took the case in hand.

"It can't be possible," it cried to the woman.

"Yes, it is true," she said.

"Why, don't you know that he killed your sister?"

"I know he did."

"And you are going to marry him, in face of that?"

"Yes."

"Well, he'll kill you."

"Oh, no, he won't kill me"—there was a peculiar light in her eyes that puzzled them.

"What can you want to marry such a man for?" they cried, coming back to the original question.

"To keep the children. If I don't marry him, some one else will, and those children will go out of my hands."

Her devotion to the motherless brood had been past praise. There was nothing more to be said, and if there had been it would have availed nothing, for the sister had a mind of her own. She was one of those handsome women, who walk this earth like queens, and to whom lesser folk defer.

She married, and lo! the neighborhood was agog once more, for strange stories came floating from out that handsome house, and it appeared for a time that instead of his killing her she was like to kill him.

I remember one tale in particular, which my mother who, by the way, was no gossip, and was as peaceable as a barnyard fowl, was in the habit of rehearsing before a chosen few, occasionally, with a quiet relish that was amusing, considering the fact that ordinarily any comment on her neighbors' affairs was alien to her. It appeared that after a short wedding trip, during which the bridegroom had several times shown the cloven foot, the couple returned to their domicile. Probably the maids who had lived there for some years and were devoted to the new wife, had been warned of what was coming. At all events, they accepted everything as a matter of course.

Upon the evening of the married pair's return, a handsome dinner was served. The train was a trifle behind time; the day had been cold, and several other untoward circumstances had conspired to let loose the bridegroom's natural depravity. An overdone roast served to touch off this inflammable material.

"—— these servants!" he exclaimed; "I'll kick every one of them through the front window! Look at that roast!"

The doors being now open, a perfect storm of ugly, evil tempers poured forth.

At such times as these it was the custom of wife number one to shiver, shrink, implore—weep, then take the offending roast from the room, and replace it by something else which most likely was hurled at her, in the end.

The present Mrs. Daemon neither shivered nor shrank. She knew what to expect when she married this man, and she was ready. The guns were loaded and aimed, and they went off, and presto! the enemy lay dead on the dining room floor.

Instead of a roast beef solo, there was a duet, Mrs. Daemon's feminine soprano rising above her husband's masculine roar. She agreed with what he said as to the disposition of the servants, only adding that she intended to hang them all, before he put them through the front window.

"To insult us during our honeymoon with such a roast," she cried; "and look at this gravy! It's even worse!"

And with one swift stroke of her hand she sent the gravy bowl flying from off the table on to the handsome carpet.

"In Heaven's name, what are you about?" he bawled.

"Do you suppose I'd offer you such gravy; it ought to be flung in their faces."

He gasped and stammered; thought of the recent wedding and regretted it; but he was married now, and to an awful shrew!

Soon after dinner they repaired to the drawing room. In turning from the fireplace he stumbled against a large, elegant vase.

"Confound that thing!" he exclaimed, "I always did hate those vases that set on the floor."

"So do I!" she chimed in, and putting out her foot with an expressive jerk, she kicked it over, and broke it into a hundred fragments.

"Do you see what you've done?" he cried, "have you forgotten that that vase was a present from me?"

"No, I haven't, but we both hate it, and what's the use of keeping it?"

This was but the beginning; from that time on, let him but murmur against a dish, and it was flung on to the floor; torrents of abuse were poured upon the head of a maid with whom he found fault; some of the handsomest furniture in the house was broken, the moment it gave offense to him. In no vehemence was he alone—his wife's anathemas and abuse joined and exceeded his, until—he had enough of it—an overdose, in fact, and erelong he turned a corner— came out of Hurricane Gulch into Peaceful Lane, and he hoped the latter would know no turning. The servants whispered of times when he would tell his wife of guests invited to the house, and entreat her not to make a scene while they were there.

Sixteen years have gone by, and this woman is still above ground; stranger still the man is alive as well; and strangest of all, they are still under the same roof. Indeed, if report and appearance are to be trusted, Mr. Daemon is a model husband, and Mrs. Daemon's sudden and amazing temper has spent itself and left her a person of spirit indeed, but in nowise unamiable, and least of all, an ugly character.

No one who saw them walk past me, arm in arm, that morning, on their way to the wreck, would have dreamed of their past.

Truly, man is a harp, and truly, woman does the harping.

IV

I have been wandering about to-day in an apparently aimless fashion, but in reality "musing upon many things." Our horror of shiftlessness, and our realization of the responsibilities of life, and of the important work Providence has kept saving up for us, or perhaps "growing up" for us, like Dick Swiviller's future mate, is expressed in the fact that if we take an hour's leisure, anywhere betwixt sunrise and sunset, we feel under bonds to explain the matter not only to our own souls, but also to those other souls who live adjacent, and take an everlasting interest in ours.

Consequently, I told myself this day that I was not well—that I had been overdoing, and that I had best "go easy for a spell." After which concession to my interior governor, I proceeded to apologize to my neighbors; to call my dogs—not to apologize to them, but to solicit their company—and then to hie me away to the lake, remembering to walk feebly as long as I was in sight.

I didn't go down to the beach, but plunged into the cool, comforting heart of a ravine; fathomed its depths, with a feeling of delightful seclusion, and came out on the thither side, to find myself in the glowing October woods.

Ill? I never felt better in my life! Good, rich streams of blood coursed through my veins, and painted a warm tint in my cheeks. At that moment I hope I looked a trifle like Nature, who was in the height of her being; in a sort of tropical luxuriance, like a beautiful woman at the very summit of maturity and perfection.

I put out my hands toward a clump of sumach—I was not cold, but its brilliant warmth lured me as does a glowing fire. It permeated my very being, and set my soul a-throbbing.

There had been rain, and then warmth, and October had caught all the prismatic colors of the drops of water, and was giving them forth with Southern prodigality. The birds bent over the swaying daisies, and sang soft love-notes into their great, dark eyes, while I looked on in an ecstasy of wonder and delight—the gold of the daisies, the gold of the sunlight, and the glow in my heart, seeming in a way all one—part and parcel of the munificence and cheering love of the Father. It is a glorious world, and it is glorious to live therein. The very air about me—the air I was breathing in, seemed to palpitate color and brilliant beauty.

I talked to Duke about it, and he looked around him with a certain air of admiration depicted on his noble, fond old face. Fanchon was frivolous, as usual, and wanted to be running giddily about, hunting rabbits and the like; but I made her sit beside me, for it seemed a desecration every time the October silence of those woods was broken by aught save the dropping of a ripened nut, or the whirr of a homing bird.

It was at the close of this mellow day that I sat in my library alone, before a hickory fire. Alone, did I say? Nay, Mrs. Simpson sat before me in the opposite rocker. You could not have seen her, or heard her, but she was there, and was complaining of Mr. Simpson, saying he rarely ever invited her to go anywhere; and as she talked I recalled a certain evening when I had been her guest—included in an invitation to attend a spectacular entertainment given by the country club, at a spot some distance from our homes, and I said:

"Mrs. Simpson, I can offer you some recipes which I warrant you will work infallibly; but they are like the recipe for determining the interior condition of eggs, which says, put them in water; if they are bad they will either sink or swim—I have forgotten which. Now try this recipe I am about to give you, and it will either make Mr. Simpson unwilling to take a step in the way of recreation without you, or it will make him stalk forth by himself, as lonely as a crocus in early March—I have forgotten which; but try it often enough, and you will learn."

Recipe.

"Fail to be ready at the appointed time, and keep him waiting until he is either raging or sullen; cudgel or dragoon the children until their tempers are well on edge. Then complain of the gait taken by Mr. Simpson in order to catch the train; declare frequently when aboard that you are tired out, and are sorry you came. After you reach the place, remark every now and then that you don't think the entertainment amounts to much, and that you do think it was a piece of extravagance to have given such a price for tickets to so-inferior an exhibition. Next, declare that you feel a draft, and are catching your 'death of cold;' interlard all this with frequent directions to the children— admonitions and complaints, and derogatory remarks about Mr. Simpson's appearance, and wonder—oft-expressed and reiterated, and put in the form of questions which you insist upon his answering, as to why he didn't wear his other suit of clothes. Finally, wind up the whole affair, by wishing you were in bed, and announcing your opinion that the trip didn't pay, and you are sure it will make you and the children ill.

"Try this faithfully, and it won't fail to accomplish something decided."

One more recipe.

I was talking to Mrs. Purblind now; Mrs. Simpson had had her fill, and gone home; and Mrs. Purblind had taken her place.

You couldn't have seen her—but that doesn't matter.

Recipe.

"This is for making a man love to stay at home with you, and inducing him to be cheerful and companionable, or for making him flee your presence as one would flee a plague-stricken city: I've forgotten which, but you will soon discover, if you try it persistently.

"Talk on disagreeable themes, talk persistently and ceaselessly; never let up; the more tired he may be the more steadily you must talk, and the more irritating your theme must be. Go to the gadfly; consider her ways and be wise. Buzz, buzz, buzz; sting, sting, sting.

"On his worst nights, always select his relatives for your theme; harp upon their faults; their failures in life; their humiliations; the unpleasant things people say of them. Then if he waxes irritable, express surprise; remind him how he used to talk against these same relatives, and how much trouble he gave them when he lived at home; add that it's plain now that he has combined with his relatives against you, and that you should be surprised if he and they didn't effect a separation. If he is still in earshot, pass on to what he once told you, beginning each remark with:

"You said that——

"And then proceed to point out wherein and howin he has utterly failed to make good his promises. Further, if he is still in the house, enlarge upon the change you have noted in his conduct toward you—how devoted he used to be, and how selfish he has become. Next, tell him how well-dressed other women are, and how little you have on.

"By this time, if not sooner, he will remember that he has night work clamoring for him at the office, or that his presence at the club is absolutely necessary, and it would be well for you to conclude your remarks by observing that if he bangs the front door so hard every time he goes out, he will loosen the hinges."

"Well now," said Mrs. Purblind—the invisible Mrs. Purblind (she always would listen to reason, which is more than could be said for the visible creature of that name), "well now, I know well enough when I go on that way, that it isn't best to do it; but the Evil One seems to enter me, and I get going, and I couldn't stop unless I bit my tongue off."

"Bite it then," I said, "and after that, jump into the lake; were you once there, your virtues would float, and your husband would love them; but alive, your virtues are beneath water, and your nagging is always on top."

"But what is one to do? Supposing all these things are true—supposing you suffer from all these wrongs."

"Did you ever right a wrong by setting it before your husband in this way, and at these times?"

"No."

"Did you ever improve your condition?"

"No. But what would you do?"

"Shut up. Dip deep into silence. In the first place, when you find you have poor material, take extra care in the cooking; study the art; use all the skill you can acquire, and finally, if that won't do, if it positively won't—if you can't make a decent dish out of him, open the kitchen door, and heave him into the ash-barrel, and the ash-man will cart him away."

I have traveled a little in my life, and have been entertained in various households. I have seen wives who deserve crowns of laurel, to compensate for the crown of thorns they have worn for years; but I have seen others, who had thorns about them indeed, but they themselves were not on the sharp end. Some of these stupid, ignorant women fancied they were doing everything possible to make home pleasant, and wondered at their failure. There they sat, prodding their husbands with hat-pins, and grieved over the poor wretches' irritability.

I recall a conversation I once overheard. The husband arrived just at dinner time. The wife heard him come in, and called to him in a faint, dying voice, from the top of the stairway—

"George, is that you?"

The answer was spiritless.

"Yes."

The wife came downstairs.

"Well, then, we can have dinner. I don't know that it's ready, though; Bridget has had a toothache all day, and she's just good-for-nothing."

All this in the same faded tone of voice.

The husband passed into the parlor, and began to read the paper.
The weary tongue of his feminine partner wagged on, in a dreary sort of way.

"I think these girls are so foolish; they haven't a bit of pluck. I've been trying to persuade her to go to the dentist's and have her teeth out, but she won't. I'm just tired to death to-night, and there's no end to the work; Bridget has been moaning around all day—why her teeth——"

"Oh, bother her teeth!"

"Why, don't you care to hear anything that goes on at home, George?"

"I don't care to hear about teeth that go on at home; Bridget's teeth especially. I don't care a rap for the whole set."

"How cross you are to-night, George! when I'm so tired, too. Johnnie, your face is dirty, go and wash it; be quick now, for it's time for dinner. I don't know that Bridget will ever call us. She's probably sitting out in the kitchen, nursing her teeth; why she has five roots there, and all of them so inflamed that——"

"Bother her roots, I say!"

"George, you are extremely irascible, but that's the way; I get no sympathy at all."

"Not when you want it by the wholesale for Bridget's roots."

"Well, what should we talk about? I don't see how we can ever have conversation in the home, if you won't listen to anything."

And so they went on—the tired husband, moody and irritable, and the tired wife, loquacious about matters of no interest. I felt sorry for her who spake, and him who heard.

A husband worn out with the cares and worries of an unsatisfactory business day, and a wife harrassed and fretted by overwork and petty annoyances, could succeed in talking pleasantly together only by the use of will-power and principle. It would require a big effort, but the effort would pay. It would be one of the best investments a married pair could make. The returns would be quick and large. I wonder more don't deposit in this bank.

V

I had not forgotten Mr. Chance. This fact annoyed me excessively, since I saw that he had forgotten me. A forgotten man may remember a woman, and preserve his self-respect, if not his merriment; but when a forgotten woman remembers a man, that is quite another thing. Not that I was brooding over Mr. Chance—far from it; I thought very little of him, in one way, for I frequently saw him with Miss Sprig; but in spite of all that, I could not quite forget the impression he made upon me the day those boys killed the gay little squirrel, and again the day the poor mother went down into the deep, dark water with her child held close to her agonized heart. The feeling I experienced for him on that awful day, was unique in my history. I had never been an impressionable girl as far as men were concerned—I was not an impressionable woman. For me to carry the thought of a man home with me—for me to dwell upon this thought, and above all to take pleasure in dwelling upon it, meant more than it would have meant for some women. That was as far as the matter had gone, but it was far enough—too far, considering his evident indifference, and I was humiliated, for the first time in my life, over my attitude toward a man. This mortification induced me to treat Mr. Chance even more coldly than I should have done ordinarily, though his trifling with Miss Sprig would have called forth some coolness of conduct under any circumstances.

I had abundant opportunity to express myself in this way, for Mr. Chance's night work necessitated late rising, and I saw him to speak to him almost every morning. Indeed, I took some pains to be in my garden during the forenoon, and from this vantage ground I could not only see much that took place between himself and Miss Sprig, but I also had opportunity to speak with him as he passed my house, on his way to the train.

Sometimes Miss Sprig walked to the station with him. He evidently absorbed much of her time and thought, and she evidently regarded him as her latest victim, for she made him a common subject of talk, and her entire acquaintance had the pleasure of hearing the foolish things he did and said. She always represented him as deeply in love with her; I have no doubt she really thought that he was.

For my own part, I cared very little whether he was in love, as it is called, or not. If he had succumbed to such a shallow-pated, bold, common girl, I felt contempt for him, and this contempt was deepened when I realized that he might be trifling with her. In any event it mortified and angered me to think he had been seen with me; (he had often called upon me and we had been out together several times), and that the old neighborhood gossips had coupled our names. Now it would be reported that Miss Sprig had cut me out; if I was pleasant toward him, they would wag their foolish old heads, and whisper about my efforts to win him back; if I was cool, they would shake these same empty pates, and prattle about my wounded affections. It was one of those cases where you can't possibly do the right thing—I mean the thing that will silence the clacking tongue: consequently, as luck would have it, I plunged into the worst possible course I could have taken, for when Mrs. Catlin, who lived catacorner from me, and who watched me as a cat watches a mouse, said something one day about Mr. Chance's feeling bound to pay attention to Mr. Purblind's cousin, as long as she was visiting there, and that she knew such a girl wasn't to his taste, and she was sure he would come to his senses soon, I was so angry that I lost control of my temper, and all control of my wits, and blazed out with:

"It's none of my business or concern whom he pays attention to, and for my part I think they're well mated."

Whereupon, realizing I had made a perfect fool of myself, and that this speech of mine would go the rounds of the suburb, and I could never erase it from the village mind—not if I lived a hundred sensible years, I had much ado to withhold myself from seizing a pot of bachelors' buttons that stood near, and breaking the whole thing over Mrs. Catlin's idiotic skull.

It was on top of this pleasant interview with Mrs. Catlin, that Mr. Chance came over, and asked me to attend a concert that evening with himself and Miss Sprig, and he very narrowly avoided receiving the bachelors' buttons that Mrs. Catlin had but just escaped.

I strode indoors, and began packing some of my effects, for I was resolved to move that day, or the next. Not because I had discovered I had such fools for neighbors—I had always known that—but because I had just discovered that they had a fool for a neighbor.

Worldly considerations prevailed with me, and I took out the Penates that I had slammed into a trunk, mended their broken noses, and set them in place once more; but I hid myself away for several days, much as Moses was hidden, but for a less dignified reason.

After a time, I cooled off, and decided to accept the world as it stood, and not to rage because the millennium did not come before I was fitted to enjoy it.

Mrs. Purblind ran over one afternoon, and I could see that she was far from happy. I had noticed for some weeks various changes in the direction of improvement, in her care of her husband and household. I had also noticed that Mr. Purblind's conduct did not keep pace with these improvements, but I fancied Mrs. Purblind was not sharp enough to see or sensitive enough to care. In this it seems I erred, as I have in one, or perhaps two, other directions during my life.

As Mrs. Purblind, for the first time since I have known her, didn't seem to care to talk, I took up a book at random, and began reading aloud. As luck would have it, I stumbled into some passages descriptive of the ideal home, and before I could stumble out again, the poor woman burst into tears. I suppose that tender little sentence served as the key that unlocked the floodgates. As soon as her grief had spent itself, she apologized, and ascribed her tears to bad news in a letter or something, and shortly afterward left. I watched her walking down the street, until my eyes were too dim to see her. It grieved me sorely that the cause of her sorrow was so deep, and so delicate that I could not offer her my sympathy. Her tears were piteous to me, and I wanted to take her to my heart, and tell her how sorry I was for her; but to do that would have been to take advantage of her moment of weakness, and that I could not—must not do. So I let her go from me with merely a few commonplace expressions of regret that she had received disturbing news, while all the time my heart was aching in unison with hers, and I kept her with me in thought, all day.

I went down to the lake directly after dinner; several things were troubling me, and I wanted to lay my puzzled head on Mother Nature's bosom.

My run down the steep sides of the bluff set the blood to coursing smartly through my veins, and a new and more cheerful stream of thought to flowing.

I was tired that night, and it was a luxury to lie flat upon my back on the beach, listening to the rhythmical thud of the big, long wave at my feet, and the song of the stars overhead. There is something unspeakably tranquillizing in the studded dome of heaven; there is also something unspeakably sad. It bends over the struggling, yearning, aching human heart, as a mother, who has attained that peace which is the outgrowth of suffering, bends over the passion, the sobbing, and the despair of her child.

"Hush, hush, it is all for the best."

"I cannot—will not bear it!"

"Hush, you know not what you say. God's hand is in it all."

"There is no God in this, or if there is, He hates me!"

"Ah, my child, He loves you with unutterable love, and pities with unutterable pity. Yet a little while, and the day shall shine upon you; then you will know—a little while."

I turned from the great vault above me, and looked out upon the restive waters, and as I turned I saw a shadowy Mrs. Purblind sitting beside me on the beach, and questioning with sad eyes and heart, the stars that bent to listen.

"I have tried," she said; her face, usually so thoughtless, tear-stained, and quivering.

"Yes, I know you have tried," I answered; "I have seen that!"

"But he is just the same."

"Yes, and will be for a long time, and you will have to go on trying for years, if you want to carry him back to the old days," I said.

"That's one of the hardest things in all the world!" she cried passionately, "if we stop doing right—the right stops with us, but if we stop doing wrong and begin to do right, the wrong goes on."

"Not for always," I said, looking up to the stars.

"Oh, for so long!"

The great dome rich with gems, and deep with peace, bent over her, and by and by her sobs ceased.

"You are trying, I know," I reiterated, "but you don't understand—you can't, for you have only a woman's nature."

"What should I have, pray?"

"A woman's, and a man's, and a child's, to be a perfect wife and mother; that is, you must be able to comprehend them all. Your husband came home cross to-night."

"Yes, irritable toward us all, and I so hoped to have everything pleasant this evening."

"He, too, had his hopes to-day, and they were flung to the ground, and broken before his eyes."

"What do you mean?"

"The special agent of a company that he has for a year been working to get, has been in town."

"Yes, I know."

"Yesterday this agent led him to suppose he was to be the favored one. All to-day he has been working toward that end, and near night he heard that this man had gone, without even saying good-by. You remember that Mr.

Purblind left home in a hurry this morning, with scarcely a
bite of breakfast; he took very little luncheon, and——"

"Well, we had dinner at the usual time, if he'd said he was
hungry, I'd have hurried it."

"He was not hungry—he was much more than that. Did you
ever see a vessel whose fuel is well-nigh exhausted drag
herself into port? What is the first thing to be done?"

"I don't know—replenish her?"

"Yes, put coal on board. Now when I saw your husband
walk up to his front door, I said to myself, he needs
coaling. A good home should be a good coaling station;
remember that."

"But what of me?" she asked with some impatience, "I, too,
have my worries and exertions—do I never need coaling?"

"Frequently," I answered.

"Well, who is to coal me, I should like to know?"

"Yourself."

"That's rather one-sided, I think. Why shouldn't my
husband look to that?"

"My dear," I said earnestly, "I never knew but one man
who saw when his wife needed coaling, and attended to her
wants. When he died (for the gods loved him), it was found
that his shoulder-blades were abnormally large—at least so
the doctors said, but I knew all the time that his wings had
budded."

"Well, this life is too much for me," murmured Mrs. Purblind drearily.

"Then don't attempt the next."

"I shan't, if I can help it, and yet I'm like to soon, for Mr. Purblind's mother is coming on a visit to us, and I know she'll worry the breath out of me."

"Don't let her."

"How can I help it?"

"By keeping the peace with her."

"Oh, I've tried that before; I've done everything I could for her, and deferred to her, and ignored myself until I seemed to fade out of existence, but it didn't work."

"Oh, yes, it did, for it made her ten times as troublesome as before."

"It certainly did, but what do you mean?"

"I mean that a mother-in-law is like a child, in that she is spoiled by having her own way."

"But what can I do?"

"Walk calmly on, doing the best you can, but recognizing your own authority and dignity, and finally she will come to recognize it. Be mistress of your own household, and director of your own children—all this quietly and pleasantly, but without wavering, and in the end she will respect and probably admire you, though she will never think you do just right, or are just the woman who ought to have married her son."

"But I've always been in hopes of making her love me as she loves her own daughter."

"That is what every romantic woman starts out with, but by and by, in the storm and stress of domestic life, that ideal is cast overboard, as a struggling ship throws its extra cargo over the rail."

"Why is it, I wonder, a man never fights with his father-in-law. Men are said to be naturally pugnacious."

"That's a mistake, my dear; a man would go several miles any day to avoid a fuss; it is we women who delight in scraps. A man occasionally has a little set-to with the girl's father, before he gains his consent to the engagement, but once he's married, it's the old lady he has to train for, or I should say who trains for him, because as a general thing it is she who gives battle, not he. The real conflict, however, takes place between the two women—the wife and her mother-in-law. If you want to see 'de fur fly,' as the darkies say, you must always come over to the feminine side of the house. Then you'll have your fill of explanations, expostulations, and recriminations."

"Well, certainly I never had any trouble with my father-in-law."

"Trouble! Do you know what I'd do, if I had a troublesome father-in-law?"

"No—murder him?"

"Murder him, indeed! Woman, have you no mercantile instinct? That would be like killing the goose that lays the golden egg. Why, the first showman would take the old gentleman off my hands, and pay me a handsome price for him. You must know that a troublesome father-in-law is so rare that the public would flock to see him. But you couldn't get anything for a troublesome mother-in-law. There are too many families trying to get rid of them, at any price. The sale of parents-in-law is governed by the same laws as other commodities, and these interfering, mischief-making mothers-in-law have become a drug in the market."

"Well, there is Mrs. Earnest, her mother-in-law is a jewel."

"Ah, now you mention a most valuable piece of property, for a woman like that—who models her conduct on the pattern of Aunt Betsey Trotwood, in David Copperfield's household, is a jewel of such magnitude and brilliancy, that she will some day be seen sparkling in Abraham's bosom, from a distance of millions of miles."

"Well, how would you cook mothers-in-law?"

"Make a delicious dish of your husband and then take a pinch—a good pinch—of mother-in-law, and throw her in as 'sass.' Speaking of this, remember that too many cooks spoil the broth, and wife and mother-in-law combined generally make a pretty mess of the husband."

VI

I was feeling a trifle dull and heavy one afternoon, and after several vain efforts to do good work, decided that a vigorous tramp would set my blood to flowing, and the wheels of my thinking mill to revolving. So out I started toward the lake, as usual. There had been a storm off the Michigan shore, and we were just beginning to get evidence of it, in the big waves that were tumbling on the beach, I like the lake in this mood—in any mood, indeed, but especially when it is rough and wild.

After quite a brisk tramp along, or near the beach, I turned back; but before going home again, I wished to come in closer contact with the tumultuous waters. At risk of being wet by the spray, which the waves were tossing on high, much as an excited horse tosses the foam from his chafing mouth, I climbed around the little bathing house, set on the shore end of the pier, and then boldly walked out, and took my seat in the midst of the tumult.

The passion of the lake was magnificent; far out—as far as eye could stretch—there were oncoming waves; the clan was gathering, and all in battle array. What an overwhelming charge they made! Surely no one could resist that onslaught. There was no deliberation, as was usual with a moderately heavy sea; no calm, inevitable heaving of the water; no steady rising, ever higher and higher, until it crested, curved, and fell with a boom. There was nothing of this to-day; no preparation; everything was ready; the warriors, armed and mounted, were already making the attack.

For a time I gloried in it all; even the anger of the waves was more admirable than terrific in my sight. It seemed as though they interpreted my boldness as defiance, and accepted the challenge. From near, from far, they were coming, and all upon me, or if that is taking too much to myself, they were making their attack upon the shore, meaning to claim it for their own, and incidentally to sweep me, a poor, insignificant atom, from their sight.

By and by I found myself oppressed with the desolation of the scene. As the day waned, and the chill that foreshadows night fell upon me, or rather rose upon me, from the cold waters, I began to feel lonely and unprotected. The waves looked so hungry, so cruel; they reached out and up toward me; they encircled with the inevitable, as with a relentless fate. I began to be afraid of them, and I rose to go back to shore.

Unlike the ocean, the lake is fixed; but that day the increase of the waves, in height and fury, had the effect of a rising tide. I realized that it would be very difficult for me to get off the pier alone, and I was more than relieved to see Randolph Chance, who had come down for a look at the lake before taking his train to the city. He joined me without trouble; a man can perform those feats so easily, whereas a woman is physically hampered.

"You're in rather a bleak place, Miss Leigh," he said.

"Yes, I have just begun to realize that."

"Oh, well, we'll manage to get off safely; but you mustn't mind a little wetting. Just give yourself to me, and we'll be on shore in a minute."

I gladly did as he bade me; it was luxury just then to have some one as strong and capable as he take the reins. He led me around the bathing house, and then lifted me from the pier. As he set me safely on the shore, his eyes met mine, and his look was a revelation to me. I was, for a moment, too startled to think, and the strangest sensation I ever experienced crept over me. If a look could speak, Randolph Chance—but I did not put it into words—not then, at least, but it was all very strange to me—most inexplicable.

We walked on quietly, both, I dare say, feeling our silence to be a trifle awkward. It was for this reason that I decided to shorten the time of our being together, by stopping at the house of a friend. The wetting I had received from the waves did not amount to anything for one so hardy as myself, so I was not deterred on that account.

The house where I stopped was a pleasant resort for me. Both Mr. and Mrs. Bachelor were interesting people. I had known Mr. Bachelor for fifteen years. He had once been one of our young men, as the saying is, young merely in the sense of being single, not in actual years, for at the time I met him he was nearer the forty than the thirty line. Nature seemed to have marked him for single—cussedness, I had almost said, from the first. He was no favorite with any set, being grumpy, fussy, and peculiar. But five years after he rose into sight above my horizon he married a most sensible, lovely woman; not a child, by the way, for she was almost forty; and in less than no time, it seemed to us, had a family of four children about him, one following the other so closely that the predecessor was all but overtaken. At first we said among ourselves that he must have borrowed these infants, and stuck them up in his home for appearance's sake, in some such manner as the proprietor of a summer hotel once stuck a number of trees in his grounds, to make a sandy, barren spot seem fertile and enticing. But by and by we became convinced that these little human shoots were his very own, not alone because they evinced some disagreeable crotchets similar to his, but also because of the love he bore them, and the change they wrought in his character and life. Even around court the man was regarded differently; warmth and esteem being extended him now in place of the dislike he had formerly aroused. He had never ceased to be a study to me, and a certain flavor of romance hung about his home—a delightful flavor, that made it an attractive visiting spot. So it was with considerable pleasure that I called upon this particular day.

I was shown into the parlor—a comfortable room, back of which was a most home-like apartment, called the study. As I sat there, awaiting Mrs. Bachelor's coming, I noticed that her husband's desk, which stood in the center of the study, was strewn with dolls, and paraphernalia closely related thereto. My observations were interrupted by the entrance of Mrs. Bachelor, who welcomed me in her cordial, cheery way. A minute later Mr. Bachelor came in, and gave me what was for him, a most friendly greeting. He excused himself in a little while, and went into his study. He had, so his wife explained, been ill with a cold for a day or two, and had been working at home the while, to make ready for the approaching trial of an important case.

Upon his entering the study, a scene occurred which I shall endeavor to give you as near to the life as possible. As a matter of course he steered directly for his desk, and his eye immediately fell upon a quantity of grandchildren, variously disposed thereon.

"Well, I declare!" he exclaimed; "if this isn't outrageous!" and he gathered up the whole crop—there were fully a dozen dolls, in all stages of development, and much doll furniture, and toggery of all kinds.

After dumping the obnoxious elements on to a divan, he returned to his desk, and with much grumbling sorted out his law-papers, and went to work. But soon after he had cleared his visage, as it were, his small daughter—a pretty child, four years old—ran into the room hugging two puggy puppies, and two kittens of tender age. It did not take her long to grasp the situation. Running to the divan, she uttered a series of cries, indicative both of alarm and displeasure.

"What—what—what is the matter?" said Mr. Bachelor, who had probably forgotten his offense by this time.

"You naughty papa!" cried the child; "what did you disturve my dollies for?"

"What did you put them on my desk for?" queried her father indignantly; "the idea! I haven't a spot on earth I can call my own."

"You've just mussed their best frocks all up," continued the child, who, without paying the slightest attention to her father's vigorous protest, was rapidly replacing her family, puppies, kittens, and all, on the desk.

"I tell you I can't have them here! I have important papers around, and I must be allowed to work in peace. Take them off!"

He started to sweep them on to the floor, but the little girl uttered a shriek.

"Papa, papa, don't," she screamed. Then, as he desisted, she added, "They've just dot to be here—it's the bestest, highest table, and the little doggies and kitties can't jump off, and I'm doing to have a tea-party with Mamie Williams. You must put your nasty old papers somewhere else."

"This is an outrage!" he exclaimed, standing up and declaiming as if he were in court; "this is imposition run riot; it has reached a climax, and I'll endure it no longer. Evidently I have no rights that even the smallest and youngest in the household is bound to respect. It is a notorious fact that I am ruled with a rod of iron, and that even this baby of the family flouts me. I say I will stand it no longer. I have been held with a tight rein, and a curb bit, but I will turn at last."

In his excitement, his metaphors became confused, horses and worms being all mixed up in a heap.

"Take the desk, take the whole of it, and to-morrow I shall leave the house! I shall go back to my bachelor quarters, where I once lived in peace."

The child regarded him seriously, from out her great, brown eyes.

"Don't go away, papa," she said at last, "you may have a little of your desk, if you won't take too much. I didn't mean to be cross at you," she added, with a pathetic quiver of her lip.

"Well, well!" exclaimed the father hastily, "there, there!" and he laid his hand softly on her curly little head, "I guess we'll get on somehow; if I can have a part of the desk, that'll answer. It's big enough for two, I guess."

And he began moving his papers around.

"Not there, papa," said the little tyrant; "no, that's the sunny side, and little bowwow must be there, 'cause he's dot the badest cold, and the kitties haven't dot but little weeny eyes yet, and they must be where it's most lightest."

"Well, well, well, where may I sit? I must get to work."

"You may sit right there, and you mustn't fiddet, 'cause you'll upset dolly's crib, if you do."

Soon he was safely bestowed, off on one side, and as he obediently kept to his limitations, all proceeded happily.

During this domestic scrimmage, Mrs. Bachelor went on chatting in her lively, pleasant fashion with me, never betraying, in any way, that she overheard the scene in the study. I was so occupied with it, that I could pay no heed to her remarks; but she was a wise woman, and knew that her husband was being cooked to a delicious turn, and that any interference on her part, would spoil the dish. I have since learned that occasionally, when she sees that the fire is really too hot for him, she comes to his rescue.

"If he sputters and fizzes, don't be anxious; some husbands do this till they are quite done."

Evidently Mrs. Bachelor has studied her cook-book.

VII

The little touch of sentiment that flashed, as it were, from Randolph Chance as he lifted me off the pier, was presently blotted, as far as effect upon me was concerned, by the return of Miss Sprig to the Purblind household, and the renewal of his attentions to her. At least I regarded them as renewed, and I coldly turned my back upon him, and let him go his way, without further thought or speculation.

I was daily becoming more interested in another acquaintance—Mr. Gregory, a man of years, whom I had known for some time. He had been a visitor at our house when my parents were living, and had, from time to time, shown me friendly attentions since their death. He frequently invited me to places of entertainment, something Randolph Chance seldom did, and in many ways contributed to my comfort and happiness. Single women are very dependent upon their men friends for pleasures of this sort; few of them care to go out at night alone, and even when they go in company with each other, the occasion lacks a zest which belongs to it when a woman has an escort. It is strange that many men—many of those who believe in the dependence of women, fall into the selfish habit of going alone to theater, concert, and lecture, and so force the women of their acquaintance into a position which their sentiments would seem to deprecate.

While in no way obtrusive, or gushing in his attentions, Mr. Gregory was most thoughtful and kind, and few women are without appreciation of conduct of this type.

Life flowed on with me with a quiet current. I was not a woman to make scenes with myself or others, and my circumstances were such as to permit of an undisturbed tenor of way.

One bright afternoon, just as I returned from a long walk, Mrs. Purblind ran over to see me, and soon afterward, Mrs. Cynic dropped in. I never could bear this latter woman; something malevolent seems to emanate from her; something that is more or less unhealthful to the moral nature of all who come in contact with it, just as the miasma from a swamp is poisonous to the physical being.

It chanced that I had just finished writing a little story, drawn from the life-page of my domestic experience; it was so endeared to my memory that I was not like to forget it, and yet, in the course of years, its outlines would probably fade a trifle if I did not take care to preserve their distinctness; for that reason I had written it out.

I ought to have had better sense than to read anything of this kind to Mrs. Cynic. In the presence of such people, that which is fresh, beautiful, and holy withers, as a cluster of dewy wild flowers is parched and killed by the hot, sterile breath of a furnace.

Usually I have some judgment in such matters, but that day all discretion seemed to take wings.

A remark of Mrs. Purblind's led up to the subject. This little woman can say ugly things at times, but they are stung out of her, as it were, by some particular hurt, and are not the expression of her real nature. She has a kind, good heart, though her judgment and tact are somewhat lacking.

We happened to be speaking of men, and something was said about their capacity for devotion, when Mrs. Purblind exclaimed:

"Devotion! the masculine nature doesn't know the meaning of the word, unless it is devotion to self."

"I must read you a little story I've written to-day. It's a true one, remember—I think I shall call it, 'Devotion'."

I went to my desk, took out the manuscript, and read as follows:

"A few years ago I owned a pair of foxhounds. Duke was the gentleman of the family, and Lady was his consort, and a lady she was indeed. I can hardly imagine a human creature of greater intelligence and refinement than this dumb beast. The attachment between herself and Duke was unique in its strength, and in its demonstration. He was fully as noble and as intelligent as she, but of a less lively, cheerful temperament. The arrival of six little Dukes was an occasion of anxiety and excitement for us all, and we were much relieved when the event was safely over, and we saw Lady and her beautiful family established in peace and comfort. Matters had run smoothly for about four or five weeks, when one day I was startled by a series of sharp yelps, which I knew came from Lady. I ran to the window, and saw the poor creature rolling in the middle of the street, in the greatest pain. By her side was Duke, and his outcries mingled with hers. The hard-hearted teamster, whose wagon had done the mischief, had driven off, but I ran to the rescue, and finally got her into the stable, where her little ones were awaiting her. She only lived a few hours, and her last act was an effort to nurse her clamorous doggies, while with her great, sad eyes she seemed to say good-by to Duke! The grief of this noble fellow was so great that we thought he would go mad. For a time he refused to let us come near her. He stood over her, licking her senseless form, pushing her gently once in a while with his head and paws, and then uttering lamentable cries when he saw that she did not move, or in any way respond; and meanwhile the tiny dogs were crawling over her, and mingling their voices with their father's deep notes of distress. It was a most pitiable sight, and we all breathed a sigh of relief when the dear old fellow permitted us to lead him off into the house, and we had an opportunity to dispose of poor Lady. I'll not try to tell of Duke's excitement and distress when he missed her; of his frantic search all over the place, and of how we followed him about, and talked to him, and tried to divert him; or how we all—Duke, and the rest of us, finally sat down in the stable, beside the motherless little family, and wept together.

"The morning after Lady died, I went out to the stable with a cup of warm milk. I had not been able to do anything with the puggy little dogs the evening before, but I thought that their sharp hunger, after several hours of abstinence, would lead them to make an effort to drink. I carried a spoon with me, also a rag to suck, and a bottle, with a nipple—all kinds of appliances, in fact.

"What was my surprise upon entering the stable, to find Duke occupying Lady's place. He was evidently trying to answer the small dogs' clamorous demand for breakfast, and it was also plain that his failure in this respect amazed and bewildered him. He lay down just as he had seen Lady do, and when this did not suffice he tried another position; failing again, he withdrew a few paces, and sat for a moment in an attitude of profound thought; returning soon, and trying another device. This resulting unfavorably, he made still another, and then another attempt, and finally, grieved to the heart, and worried by the hungry cries of the small dogs, he withdrew once more, and lifting his nose high in air, deliberately yowled.

"At this point I obtruded myself upon the scene and went up to the dear old dog, took his distressed head in my arms, and talked to him. I explained to him the difficulty of the situation; how, owing to circumstances quite beyond his control, he could not take Lady's place. I urged upon him that he must yield gracefully to his limitations; showed him my appliances, and then when I had soothed and interested him, and he had consented to desist, and let me try, I made my essay.

"It was a study for an artist—my appealing, pitying, impatient, scolding efforts to induce those unreasonable little creatures to accept a rag, or a bottle in place of a mother. I shouldn't have cared so much, that is, I could have taken longer without minding it, had it not been for Duke. His anxiety was so great, and his distress over their cries so keen, that I was quite unnerved, and as is often the case, I showed my concern by scolding and abusing the objects in whose behalf I was exerting myself.

"I was all but ready to give up, when one of the smallest and liveliest of the puppies (a feminine creature, of course) suddenly seized upon the nipple of the bottle with a lusty grip, and sucked away till she was all but strangled with milk. Her example was speedily followed by the others, but before I had gone the rounds Duke comprehended that our trials were ended, and then—well, the dignified, sad-faced old doggie took leave of his wits, temporarily, as well as his dignity. He capered, he rolled on the ground, he barked, he bayed, he played leap-frog over my head, did everything but stand on end, and very nearly that, in his joy.

"From that time on he never failed to be present when his infants were fed, and when I weaned them, and taught them to drink, he was an interested spectator; helpful too, for one time when a small dog was obdurate, he took him by the nape of the neck, and shook him thoroughly, before turning him over to me for another trial. On another occasion, the pig of the family drank too deep, as it were, from the flowing bowl, and might have been drowned had it not been for his watchful parent. Duke noticed that the small fore-quarters were plunged into the liquid dinner; he also observed that the hind quarters were slowly rising in midair. He watched all this, with his accustomed, kindly gravity, until the equilibrium was lost, and Master Pup plunged into the pearly sea. Then the startled father leaped to his feet, snatched his offspring from a milky grave, and laid him, sneezing and choking, sadder and wiser, on the sunny grass-plat to dry.

"In due time Duke recovered, in a measure, from his grief over Lady's death, and took unto himself another partner. As is usual in the case of widowers, his second choice was injudicious, for Fanchon was a giddy, young thing, that didn't have sense enough to come in out of the rain.

"But Duke saw no defects; he was all tenderness and attention.

"It was early winter, but the weather was intensely cold, and we had taken Duke and Fanchon in from the stable, and had housed them comfortably in the cellar.

"One night I was wakened out of a sound sleep by cries of distress. I called my sister and her husband, who were visiting me, and in various costumes, all hands went below. Fanchon was running about, crying and moaning, and Duke was alternately making frantic efforts to soothe her, and kiyiying in a manner that was fearful to hear. We succeeded at last in getting Fanchon to heed us, and coaxed her to settle down in a comfortable bed we made for her on the far side of the cellar, where she would have the benefit of the warmth from the furnace, and would be out of the way of the cold air which came in through a window, broken the day before.

"As soon as she was pacified, Duke was again happy, and he cheerfully lay down to rest. We retired to our rooms, and being very weary, with much sightseeing during the day, dropped into a sound sleep. The next morning I hurried down into the cellar, wondering whether I should see two dogs, or a dozen. To my surprise and dismay, I saw none at all. The cellar was silent and deserted. I opened the outer door, and with a failing heart, stepped into the clear, bitter cold of a temperature something like fifteen degrees below zero. Just around the corner of the house, in a nook slightly sheltered from the biting air, I came upon the family. Fanchon lay upon the ground, the snow carefully pushed up around her, and her clinging little ones, who were taking their breakfast. Over all—Fanchon and her puppies— covering them with his faithful body—shielding them with his never-failing love and devotion, was my noble hound— as noble, as faithful a dog, as ever man or woman loved. I called to him, and rubbed him, but all in vain, and meanwhile stupid, silly Fanchon, that had foolishly left her warm bed in the cellar, looked on with cheerful indifference, and wagged her tail."

"Well," said Mrs. Cynic, when I had concluded the reading, "that story seems to me to prove but one thing."

"And what is that, pray?" I asked, realizing I had been foolish to read such a tale to such an auditor.

"Why, the truth of Madame de Staël's remark: 'The more I see of men, the more I admire dogs.'"

That hateful woman! She always leaves me with a bad taste in my mouth. I know she springs from some corrupt ancestry. She has all the marks of inward decay upon her.

When she had gone, Mrs. Purblind and I breathed more freely.

"She doesn't believe in anything good," said Mrs. Purblind.

"No," I answered in a tone of disgust, "she has nothing within her to answer to it."

"How different she is from Mrs. Earnest," continued Mrs. Purblind; "why, you can hardly convince that woman that anyone is really mean, and goodness knows she has trouble enough to make her bitter. What a husband she's got! That man makes me so mad! He's ugly from sheer badness."

I thought for a moment, and then I assented. I really do believe that man is ugly without cause. He and his wife live at some distance from us, and I've often visited them. I should like to give you a scene to which I was witness one evening when I was a trifle ill, and lay on a divan just out of their dining room.

Mrs. Earnest is like a delicate flower that lifts its pretty face and smiles in the sunlight of love, but is bowed and broken 'neath the thunder-cloud and storm. She longs to make her home attractive, but her husband has no sympathy with this desire; to him home is merely the place where he finds food and lodging, and a safety valve for such moods and tempers as he is obliged to keep under control in the business world.

The efforts that this poor little wife makes, in her timid way, to start up pleasant subjects of conversation would move a rock to tears.

This is the scene, as I recall it—a specimen scene.

The family—husband, wife, and three little children were at dinner, as I said.

"What's been happening to-day? anything of interest?" asked the little wife.

"Not that I know of," was the gruff reply.

Silence, broken by the occasional sound of eating implements, ensued.

"Pass the bread, will you?" he said in a short tone, directly.

"See how you like this bread; we are trying the entire wheat flour. I think it's very nice tasting, and they claim it's rich in nutrition. It's warranted to make blood, bone, and muscle—brain, too, I believe. I'm going to eat several pounds a day; I may astonish the world yet."

This feeble joke was received in stolid silence, and the poor little wife crept into her shell.

After a time she peeped out again, and made another effort.

"I went to the womans' club this afternoon; Mrs. Pierson invited me. They had a very interesting meeting; they brought up the subject of smoke consumers. I never realized before how much property is ruined yearly by the smoke. It does seem as if manufacturers ought to use consumers."

At this point Bruin openly yawned, and the little wife again retired. But with astonishing elasticity of courage she issued from her shell once more, this time with the hope that a more masculine theme would meet with some response.

"They brought a petition around here to-day for us to sign. It seems there is some talk of flooring the reservoir and using it as a beer garden this coming summer, and the neighborhood has been called upon to protest against it."

"I know all about that," he growled.

"Have you signed it?"

"I have."

Again silence fell as a wet cloak upon them, and the little woman sat there racking her brains, almost depleted by this time, for the atmosphere which such a man as that creates is warranted to dry up all the intellectual juices.

One more despairing effort. The children had now left the table, so anecdotes of them were in order. Probably the poor little wife thought that this man could be wakened into attention by a story about one of his children.

"Mamie asked me where cats went to when they died. 'They don't go anywhere,' I said; 'when they die, that's the end of them.'

"'Do they turn to dust?' she asked.

"'Yes, just turn to dust,' I said.

"'Why, then,' she exclaimed, and her eyes grew as big as saucers, 'when horses run 'long the streets, are they kicking up cats?'"

All the man said was, "Umph," and the little wife's peal of merry laughter was checked, and the ha ha's grew fainter and spread farther and farther apart, until they died away altogether, and I felt like charging upon that burly, surly demon, and butting him out of the window.

"How would you serve such a man, if you were his wife?" asked Mrs. Purblind.

"Roasted!"

VIII

Mr. Gregory's attentions had become an accepted fact in my life. They were dignified and steadfast, and I received them with a certain calm pleasure. They had not, as yet, reached the point of declaration, but it was clear to me, and to everyone else, who knew anything about the matter, that they were tending thither, and my own thought had reached the point of acceptance. I had the greatest respect for him as a man; we were congenial in our tastes, and personally agreeable to one another. The position he had to offer me was a most dignified, desirable one, as he was not only a man of sterling integrity, but also a man of wealth; there was, in short, everything in favor of the alliance, and I looked upon it quietly, but with a sense of substantial, and steadfast comfort.

Such an event as a marriage cannot even in prospect, face a thoughtful woman without making a great change in her life. Mr. Gregory was that type of man who ought not to be allowed to offer himself in a direction where there was no intention of acceptance, for his character and age—he was fifty or more—forbade all thought of lightness or trifling, and gave one the assurance that any marked attention he might show, was significant. My acquaintance with him had extended over several years, and during this period there had been abundant opportunity, on both sides, for study of character.

In a quiet way, I had been arranging my affairs, preparatory to my expected change in manner of life. I had, as a matter of course, done considerable thinking during this time. I had experienced none of the rapture always associated with a romantic attachment, but I was quietly happy, and this condition was a far more natural one for me, with my cool, matter-of-fact temperament—a far more promising one, in respect to future enjoyment, I felt, than something more ecstatic.

I had seen but little of Mr. Chance for some weeks. He had called several times, but on each of these occasions, we had passed a somewhat constrained, and I thought, a rather dull evening. Just why this constraint should have crept into our intercourse when we seemed to be coming to a better understanding than heretofore, and were beginning to enjoy a warmer degree of friendship than we had known, I could not understand; but its presence was undeniable, and it spoiled everything for me, as far as he was concerned, causing me to look upon his calls in the light of a bore, rather than as a pleasure, as I once had done. Occasionally a memory of that evening when he came to my rescue, as the hungry, cruel waves gathered like wolves about me, would flit across my mind, as a shadow may flit across a sunlit hill. Once in a long while I found myself dwelling upon the look he gave me that night, and this, and the memory of his touch, as he lifted me off the pier, would dim the sunshine of my cheerfulness. I could not have explained this to myself, and I never dwelt upon the thought; whether from disinclination, or from fear, I could not tell. I only knew that I always turned from it abruptly, and passed on to my plans affecting my life with Mr. Gregory. It was quite easy to plan in this direction, for there was nothing uncertain, as there might have been in the case of a younger man. Mr. Gregory was fixed in his tastes, and way of life; I, too, at my age, had formed settled habits, and this he knew; but, fortunately, in most directions, we were in harmony, and where we were not, we had fallen into a way of making certain concessions.

So I had matters pretty well laid out; all my theories, born of years of close observation of affairs domestic, were now brought to bear on my own future. Secretly I esteemed myself a competent cook, when a husband was the dish under discussion. Mr. Gregory was not one to require any very complicated wisdom in the culinary art. A little gentle stewing; no strong seasoning; no violent changes or methods of any sort; but regularity, evenness; quiet affection; respect; comfort, and general conformance to taste and nature would be necessary, and I felt myself fully equal to it all.

Matters had well-nigh culminated, for I had received a note from Mr. Gregory asking when I would be at home to him, and saying that he had a matter of great moment to both of us, to lay before me. I set an evening, and then awaited his coming without the slightest quickening of my pulse, but with a serenity and cheerfulness that appealed to my common sense as the surest forecast of happiness.

Just at this juncture, a swift turn of the wind-cock, or some imprudence of diet, resulted in my taking cold—a most unusual procedure for me, and at the time of Mr. Gregory's call I was unable to see him, being confined to my bed, in the care of a doctor, who was fighting a case of threatened pneumonia.

Mr. Gregory expressed his sincere regret, and the next day called again, and left flowers. These attentions were repeated daily, and soon after hearing of my improvement, he wrote me a letter in which he said that which he had intended to say on the evening of the day I fell ill. He did not request a reply; in fact, he asked me to withhold my answer until I should be able to see him in person. It would have been wiser, perhaps, he said, to have postponed any word on the subject until I had recovered, but he had found it difficult to delay the expression of his feeling toward me, and hence had written.

This last rather surprised me, for Mr. Gregory had always seemed so unlikely to be swayed by impulse, or carried, in the slightest degree, beyond a point indicated by his judgment. It simply went to prove that the most regularly and smoothly laid-out man, if one may so express it, has unsuspected crooks and turns.

I had no desire to answer the letter, being perfectly able and willing to wait until I should see him. In fact, instead of hastening the time for my acceptance, I rather delayed it, for I reached a point in my convalescence, when I was able to go down to the parlor, had I so wished, and still did not.

Each day of my illness, a lovely bouquet of flowers had been left at my door. They came direct from the greenhouse, and were left without card, or sign of the giver. I had an eccentric little friend who was quite devoted to me, and was fond of keeping her left hand in darkest ignorance of the performances of its counterpart—the right hand—and I attributed this delicate and beautiful token of sympathy and affection to her; but, for some inexplicable reason, every morning when the flowers were brought to my room, and I took them in my hand, a strange feeling came over me—a feeling I had never had toward my little friend.

Over two weeks had passed, and I was downstairs in the study. My nurse had gone out, my housekeeper was busy, and I was very lonely. I was standing at the window, looking westward. The sun had gone down in regal splendor. Some fête was in progression in the sky, for the attendants of the god of day were resplendent in attire. They had been marshalled from all quarters of the heavens, and their stately and solemn procession, brilliant with the most gorgeous red, royal purple, and dazzling gold, had caused my heart to dilate with awe and reverential admiration.

The lake, stirred by the wonderful pageant, caught the many hues as they dropped from heaven, and tossed them on high in joyous, iridescent waves.

The climax of majesty and beauty was reached, and then the convocation broke up—not suddenly, but slowly, and with gracious dignity. The sun sank into the waiting arms of the unknown; the lights of heaven faded, and the clouds slowly melted into dusk.

The scene had stirred me as I am seldom stirred, and with the oncoming of night new thoughts and feelings rose from their lair, as strange and beautiful wild animals step from their caves into the deep mystery of darkness.

My neighbor next door—Mrs. Thrush, sat on her broad, vine-clad gallery, rocking her little child in her arms. By her side sat her husband, with one arm thrown across her lap. He had laid his paper down, for the daylight was fading, and perhaps his thought was too happy to stoop to daily news. Softly the little wife and mother sang; she had a sweet home voice, and no music of orchestra ever moved me as did her lullaby.

I was at that moment an intensely lonely woman. I thought of Mr. Gregory and my future, and still I was lonely.

Far away to the east there was a low, long bank of clouds like a mountain range, and as the poetry and melody of the lullaby rose from the little nest on my left, and stole into my thought, I saw a faint light above this line; then a group of mist-like clouds that moved toward me. Slowly the gray haze, tinged with soft light, began to resolve itself into shadowy forms, and my heart stood still as, in some vague way, I traced a connection between the lullaby and the vision, and realized that a message was coming to me.

I was perfectly calm, but with the calmness which is the outgrowth of an excitement so tense that it is still. As the vision floated nearer, I heard soft music—a crooning, yearning, soul-satisfying lullaby; I saw a little child, a mother, and a father. The child was as beautiful as an angel, and there was that in its face which made my eyes flood with tears, and my heart ache with yearning; the faces of the parents were too vague for me to recognize at first; then slowly, that of the mother became more distinct, and I saw myself before me—myself, a wife and mother; the visible answer to my heart's deepest, most secret cry. Still the father's face was hidden, but as the vision floated by, he turned and looked at me—the vision wife—with a look I had seen before, and I uttered a cry as I recognized Randolph Chance.

IX

As I cried out, I turned slightly and, for a moment, lost the picture. It was changed when again I saw it; Randolph Chance was still there, but he no longer advanced toward the vision wife—she had faded into mist; he came slowly toward me. There was a beautiful look on his face—I cannot describe it—it was too holy to translate into language; but I could feel it vibrate through my being until it set my very soul a-quivering. I had no power of resistance—no wish to resist. I almost think I went toward him, and he was as real to me as if he were in the flesh. I could feel him as he put his arm around my waist, and his face touched mine. The vision child had melted away; and we two were alone; I knew my heart then; I knew I loved this man.

It was all over in a few moments, but such moments as make an eternity, for they wipe out the past, even as death blots out a life, and they open a door to the future. Up to that time I had never thought that, without my knowledge or intent, my heart could slip from me—had never dreamed that I, whose life had always been most commonplace—I, who had had my share of wooing, but had never felt an extra heart-beat because of it—no, never dreamed that I, this I, so practical and sensible, could be carried off my feet by a vision. A vision, was it? Yes, and yet real, too real in some ways, since it revealed my innermost thought. A vision! And yet, even now that it had melted into air, I was clinging to it, and instead of resenting its startling revelation of self, was dwelling upon it, and in it, with a delight beyond words.

I sat there in my study, my head bent, and my hands loosely clasped in my lap, living it over and over again. Out of doors, the soft gray dusk had hushed the tired world in its arms. Within, the stillness of night had settled down upon the room. By and by the moon rose above the great waters of the lake, and on shore the trees were casting silent, solemn shadows, made visible by the soft, hazy light that lay between them. Once in a while a bird uttered its night cry, or some little brooding note, and over on the vine-clad gallery, Mrs. Thrush still crooned a lullaby to her little child, who lay asleep—soft and warm, on her mother-breast.

I was no longer lonely, no longer shut out from it all—there was the bird on its nest; the little wife and mother in her home; and I—I was very near them—akin to them. I had seen myself in my home, with my child, and my husband; I had felt his dear arms about me, and his dear face close to mine. I was no longer an alien. I, too, had a place in the heart of another.

Still I sat and dreamed, and even the ringing of my door-bell failed to rouse me: but when I heard the maid say to someone:

"She has been downstairs to-night, but I think she has gone up now, and I don't like to call her."

I started forward, saying quickly:

"No, I am here—I will see any one."

And so he came in, but it was not the one I expected. It was Mr. Gregory.

I think that he found my embarrassment on greeting him both gratifying and encouraging, but its cause was alien to his thought. I was brought back from another world, as it were, with a rude shock, and in my enfeebled condition, consequent upon a severe illness could not control myself. Indeed I did not feel that I was mistress of myself at any time during the evening.

After a word or two, which I cannot recall, I stammered out:

"I was not expecting you this evening—I had not sent for you."

"I know that you have not," he answered—then dropping his voice a trifle, he added, "I could not wait any longer—I found it difficult to wait so long as this. I hardly dared hope that I might see you this evening, but I felt I must try."

Intent upon sparing him the pain of a spoken declaration, I exclaimed:

"Oh, Mr. Gregory, don't! please don't say anything more. I am not deserving of your esteem and kindness."

He came nearer me, and his voice was at once tender and reverent, as he said:

"You are more than worthy of what I have to offer, which is myself, and all that I have."

"Don't!" I cried again; "don't say anything more! Let us imagine this unsaid!"

"Such words can never be recalled," he said gravely.

"They must be," I persisted; "I cannot accept! I have nothing to give in return!"

A look of disappointment came over his face, and if I mistake not, it was shaded with displeasure. "I hardly expected this, Miss Leigh, I have hardly been led to expect this."

"I know what you mean, Mr. Gregory," I replied, more calmly than I had spoken before; "I know that I have accepted your attentions—you have had every reason to expect a different answer. I'll not try to deceive you, or keep anything from you. I'll tell you that I have not been trifling. I have understood you for some time——"

He interrupted me here.

"Yes, you must have done so; my attentions to you could have but one interpretation, if I were a man of honor, and you knew I was that."

"I did, indeed," I exclaimed. And then my mind went, with a flash like lightning, to Randolph Chance, and I felt a sudden resentment. Had not he shown me attentions that no man of honor can bestow upon a woman, unless he wishes to make her his wife? Why had he left me in this strait? Why had he not spoken out? Why had he not claimed before the world that which he had taken such pains to win? I was uncertain about Randolph Chance; I had never been uncertain about Mr. Gregory. Why? Because I had perfect confidence in his honor. Was he not the better man—the more trustworthy? Why could I not marry him? I loved another man. A wave of shame and anger swept my face.

"I have all along been expecting to marry you. I have not been trifling," I cried out.

He stepped forward, and took my hand. It was as cold as ice.

"What is it then, Constance, that has changed you? Have I done anything since your illness to make you think less of me?"

I trembled from head to foot, and my lips were so stiff and dry that they scarce would do my bidding. I must have spoken very indistinctly.

"No—no," I said slowly; "I will tell you everything—I have done you a wrong, an unintentional wrong, but I will do penance—I have seen myself to-night—" I paused here; Mr. Gregory was a practical man; had I told him that a vision had changed my attitude, he would have thought me insane. I myself had begun to entertain doubts as to my sanity. "I know myself now," I faltered, "I know my heart—I love another man."

Mr. Gregory rose, and began pacing the floor.

"This surprises me greatly," he said at length; "there must have been another courtship—it would seem that you must have known something of how matters were tending."

"I have known nothing until to-night. There has been no courtship, in the ordinary acceptation of that word—I'll tell you all, even if it humbles me completely, as a penalty for what I have done to you. The man I love—" I could feel the blood mantling my face and neck, "has never addressed me."

Mr. Gregory paused, and looked at me.

"This is extraordinary," he said.

"It is—I know it is—it is most of all so to me, for it is wholly unlike what I have been all my life."

"Let us not talk of this any more to-night, Miss Leigh," he said, with evident relief; "I have been wrong to press this matter now, when you are hardly recovered. You are not yourself. This is something transitory, no doubt. Later on, you may feel differently."

"No, no!" I exclaimed eagerly, "now that we have begun, let us say it all. Don't—I beg of you, don't go away with a feeling that I don't know my mind. I am weak and miserable to-night—" here the tears choked my voice, and I all but broke down, "but I am miserable because I have learned my true feeling, and know that I must disappoint——"

I could not go on, and again he sat down beside me and took my hand.

"I cannot understand you," he said simply.

"I can't understand myself," I replied; "but all this is none the less real for that. I have learned of it to-night, but it has existed before; it explains many things in the past year."

"If that is the case, then I must accept your decision as final."

"It is, indeed," I answered briefly.

He rose, and walked the room in silence again; then pausing once more, he said calmly, and with no trace of anger.

"This is the disappointment of my life."

I said nothing. What could I say? To utter any platitudes about being sorry, would have been to insult him.

"A man cannot live to my age—I am fifty-two, Miss Leigh—without experiencing disappointment, but I have known nothing equal to this."

He paced the room a few moments, and then said:

"This interview must be distressing to you. I am very sorry I brought it about before you were strong and well."

"Say one thing before you go, Mr. Gregory," I cried, "only say that you don't think I have willfully misled you—say that you respect me still."

His face was stirred by a slight quiver, as a placid lake is stirred by an impulse of the evening air.

"You have had, and you always will have my deepest respect, and my deepest affection."

He took my hand silently, and then quietly left the room.

And I sat there until I heard the front door close. Then I went upstairs, but I remember nothing after reaching the first landing.

They found me lying there. They said I must have fainted.

X

I was badly upset for several days. For a time I resolutely put all thought of what had occurred from my mind, but as soon as I felt able, I sat down, with the whole matter before me, as it were, and deliberately looked it in the face. I think I never felt more inane in my life than when I remembered my folly, as I now regarded it. All that saved me from utter self-abasement was the fact that it had occurred at a time when I was at such a low ebb physically, by reason of illness. I determined to try to forget it, as speedily as possible. But, however keenly I felt the humiliation and folly of my emotion upon that strange night, it never occurred to me to waver, when recalling my decision to bring matters between Mr. Gregory and myself to an end. My refusal of him had been brought about by one cause, and only one—that I fully realized; and now that I had repudiated the cause, I might have been expected to reconsider the refusal. But I did not.

Soon after I was up and about once more, I learned that my little friend had not sent the flowers. I thought—no, I did not think! but I cherished secretly a—well, no! I cherished nothing in secret or in public!

I learned something else, soon after getting up, and this was that a story was going the rounds to the effect that Mr. Gregory had broken our engagement—and my disappointment had well-nigh occasioned me a relapse. But in a twinkling, almost before I had time to get indignant, Mrs. Catlin was running about, telling everybody that Mr. Gregory had confided in her, in strictest confidence, the truth of the matter, which was that I had ended the affair, and not he.

I was much moved by this manly act on Mr. Gregory's part. He showed his shrewdness, too; he could not announce this in public, or go to people one by one, so he confided it to Mrs. Catlin, and told her not to tell.

One Sabbath evening about ten o'clock, I began to lock up the house. Early retirement is something all but unknown to me, but that night, having no particular reason for sitting up, I was about to indulge in it as a novelty.

I raised the shade of one of the study windows, with intent to draw the bolt, but my hand paused in the act, for my eyes were captured by a scene of surpassing beauty. Fall had lately swept her gorgeous leaves one side, and closed her doors for the season, and we were now standing on the threshold of winter. The early snows are apt to be soft and clinging; it is later on, usually, when the thermometer takes a plunge downward, that they become crisp and hard. It is seldom, however, at any time of year that the atmospheric conditions are favorable to such a creation as I beheld that night. I hardly know just what is necessary to make it all— a still, moderate cold, and a very humid air are among the most important conditions, I believe.

When I stepped outside my door early in the evening, the air all about me seemed to be snow, not separated into flakes, but diffused evenly. Altogether it had the effect of a heavy white fog, and I could see even then, that it was settling in visible, palpable, feathery forms, not only upon the ground, but upon every bush and tree as well. It was a most unusual scene, and I gazed at it long and admiringly; but having no fondness for walking through soft, clinging snow, I was not enticed to sally forth, as I always am when the snow is firm and sparkling.

But by ten o'clock the temperature had changed, and in the cooler air the almost imperceptible melting of the snow had been stayed.

The white carpet that had slowly been sinking, was now stationary, and was covered by a firm crust that gleamed in the moonlight. There was no sparkle on the trees, but the feathery tufts and pinions had ceased floating to the ground, and melting into air. The scene, in all its matchless beauty, was arrested—held upon nature's canvas for a few hours, by the Master hand.

Stay in doors that night! Would I be so wicked as to turn my back, or close my eyes upon one of the most delectable scenes that ever a kind Providence spread before the soul of human creature! Would I deliberately slight such an exhibition of love and marvelous skill? Not I!

It didn't take me long to catch up hat and jacket, and with a heart that beat high, slip from my house, as a greyhound slips the leash, and hie me away.

What mattered it that the neighborhood lights were raised—a story, at least—and that the owners of all the villas near at hand, were preparing for decorous, temporary retirement. I merely pitied them for their stupidity, and went my way. I had long been a law unto myself, and while I did not believe in flaunting my independence in their faces, I none the less continued to enjoy it.

There are nights when to sleep would be the sin of an ingrate; 'twould be like gathering up the good things of Providence, and hurling them from out the window, in reckless waste. And this night was such a one.

The keen air, and the entrancing beauty about me, seemed to run in a subtle, fascinating torrent through my veins, and lend me wings. I felt as though I were buoyed up by magic hands; I hardly think I set foot on ground the whole way, and yet I must, for I was conscious of a crisp crackle of the snow at every step.

Oh, is there any sound just like it! Could our poor invalids but pitch their nostrums over the wall, and take this tonic instead!

Some friends of mine moved a while ago and drove their family stake in a spot far off from here. They are continually writing me of a region of perpetual sunshine and summer. I thought of them on this glorious night, and pitied them from the depths of my heart, as I often have, indeed, since they went out there. Theirs is the place for the extremely indigent, no doubt, but for any one who can command a dollar or so for fuel, this—this is the land of delight.

I was at no loss as to direction; our suburb was beautiful throughout, especially all along by the lake, but there was one place in particular, where art and nature had joined hands, with a result indescribable. Toward these grounds I hastened, on this particular night.

Oh, the glory of that moon! the glory of the lake! an undulating sea of waves, each crested with a feather, as soft, as snowy in the moonlight, as the tinier ones that hung upon the trees.

I ran down the winding avenue—the white fog still lingered in the deep places, but above, all was clear and glorious. Erelong I entered the Dunham's grounds. At a certain point, unmarked to the stranger's eye, a rustic flight of stairs, now strewn with dead leaves—padded with snow as well, to-night, dips down from the broad driveway. Quickly I made my way by this path, and erelong, stood upon one of the little rustic bridges spanning the ravine, and connecting with a similar flight of ascending stairs upon the other side. There I paused, and well I might. It were a dull, plodding creature indeed, who would not be spellbound by such a scene! On either hand were the sloping wooded sides of the ravine whose depths were shrouded in the mysterious whiteness of the fog; above me, a short distance in front, was the arch of the broad, picturesque bridge with which the driveway spans the hollow. The little rustic bridge on which I stood was much lower than the larger one; hence, from my position, I looked through the archway, beyond, down, and far along the ravine. Can you call up fairyland to your mental eye? It would pale before this scene—those feathery trees! that enchanting vista! I stood there drinking it in, and pitying the sleeping world. I could not, even in thought, express my delight and gratitude for being permitted to behold such beauty, but finally a familiar line leaped from my lips:

"Praise God from whom all blessings flow."

I can never forget that night; it kindled and warmed my heart with a reverential fire. If, in the course of years, my way should be overcast; if, for a time, I should let the artificial—the ignoble, clog the path, and shut me out from the light of heaven, even then I shall be saved from doubt, which is always engendered by our stupidity—the things of our own manufacture—I shall be saved from doubt by the sweet, pure, radiant memory of that winter, moonlight scene. Only a beneficent God could create such beauty.

XI

On my way back—at what dissipated hour I firmly decline
to state—I passed a home with an interesting history tacked
thereto.

The leading events were brought me by one of those active,
inquisitive little birds that find out all sorts of things, and
often fetch from great distances.

The couple who live there, though Americans, once lived in
Winnipeg, Manitoba, and it was in that place that the
husband fell to drinking. The little bird above alluded to—
the bird that acts as a kind of domestic ferret—told me that,
in the early years of their married life, the wife was of an
excitable, hysterical temperament, and given to making
scenes. Just here let me digress a moment to erect a
warning signboard. I have a friend who is busy mixing and
administering a deadly draught to her domestic happiness,
and yet does not know it. She has only been married a year,
and she uses tears and scenes, in general, as instruments to
pull from her husband the attention, affection, and devotion
she craves. The tug waxes increasingly hard, but she has
not, as yet, sense enough to see that, and desist. She cannot
realize that the success attained by such methods is but the
temporary and external beauty, which, in reality, covers a
failure of the most hopeless type, just as the flush on the
consumptive's cheek is but a pitiable counterfeit, and
covers a fatal disease.

Whether in this particular story, the report of the wife's
early blunders be true or false, there seems to be no doubt
that presently the husband grew careless and indifferent;
that scene followed scene between them, until at last he

went to drinking. Then the little wife waxed sober, thoughtful, and studied much within herself. This awful sorrow, following so closely upon the heels of her wedding-day joy, matured her judgment—her womanhood, and she began to use every skillful device to call back her husband from the dark paths he had chosen, to the light. All in vain, however; and when she realized this, after several years of heroic effort, she made one last scene, and told him she was going to leave him. Then his old-time tenderness returned—if you can compare a tenderness which was blurred and cringing, with that which was clear and manly. He begged and promised in vain, however, for she had lost faith, and a lost faith is not found again for many a day.

So she went off, and she covered all traces and signs so carefully that no anxious, heartbroken effort of his could find her. Meanwhile she wrote him frequently and regularly, and although he knew not where to send reply, it is quite likely she had word of him from some one to whom she had given her confidence in this dreary time.

And so five years passed, and at their close she walked into her home one day, and her husband—a man once more, took her in his arms, and looked his love and joy with clear, honest eyes.

They came to our city, or rather this little suburb of our city, soon afterward, and although it is well-nigh ten years now that they have been among us, there has never been a hint of trouble. Hers was a unique method, but it brought about the desired end.

Verily it would seem that for some dinners, it is best for the cook to vanish, and leave the dishes to get themselves.

I was meditating on this as I walked home that night, and the next morning, stirred by the recollection of all I had seen and felt, was moved to write out a story given me by a young man—a friend of mine, who lives at a great distance from here, on an olive ranch out of Los Gatos, California.

I wish I could give you this little tale just as he told it. I can't, I know, but I'll do my best in trying.

Mrs. Purblind dropped in just as I was reading it over to myself, before my study fire.

"Do you remember my story about Duke?" I asked.

"Yes, I liked it," she said, "though I'm not very partial to dogs."

"I have one here about horses. I've written it out as nearly as possible as my friend told it to me, but so much flavor is lost when these things change hands. Here it is, and I think that the lamentation David sang over Saul, might head it.

"A while ago we owned a couple of horses—work horses, and yet, by reason of the strength of their affections, they were lifted from out the commonplace, and enveloped with an atmosphere of romance that gave them the flavor of a story book, plumb full of princes and heroes. And by the way, Prince was the name of one of them, and he was a genuine hero, as you will see. His mate was called Nelly, and albeit she was as awkward and as angular as the ideal old maid, vastly inferior to Prince, who was a fine-looking chap, yet his admiration for her was unbounded. She cared for him, I'm sure, but she was less demonstrative; more coquettish, I would say, if she hadn't been too homely a beast to think of, in connection with such a word.

"They were brought up together; were taught by the same master; sat on the same bench, in a figurative sense; were lovers from the very first. Prince certainly had the most elegant manners; Nelly was his first thought, at all times, and his courtesy to her savored of the old school. He wouldn't go into the shed of a cold, rainy day and leave Nelly outside; but if she went in, he was more than content to follow. When it was necessary to separate them—we couldn't always work them together—we had to tie Prince with ropes and cables, as it were, to hold him fast. Nelly was less difficult to manage; at least, she would let him go out of sight without fretting, and yet, after all, she seemed easier if he were at hand. I remember, one day, he was tied in front of the house, and she was loose, grazing near by. As long as he could see her, all went well enough, but the moment she sauntered around the fence, he began first to fidget, then to paw and neigh, and finally to struggle, until in the end, he broke loose and rushed after his inamorata. And what a time he made over her! whinnying, and demonstrating his delight in a dozen different ways. She? oh, she took it coolly, but that was all feminine bosh, or coquetry on her part. She liked to have him near her well enough.

"There was an amusing thing happened one day, down in the field. Father and I were plowing with Nell. We had tied Prince to a tree, the other side of the knoll we were working on, and supposed he was fast, but to our surprise, just as we turned, after finishing a long furrow, we confronted the gentleman, tree and all, standing before us in a weak and fainting condition. He had struggled until he had uprooted the whole business, and was so used up in consequence, that he could hardly stagger, much less go into his usual hysterics over Nell. She looked as amazed as we did, and I've no doubt gave him a sound curtain lecture on his folly that night.

"One day father and Ned took Prince down into the field. Steve and I stayed up near the house, working around the vineyard. Nelly was in the stable.

"The morning was half gone, when all at once Steve happened to turn around, and look down the hill.

"'Gosh, Jack!' he exclaimed, 'the barn's afire.'

"I gave one startled look, and then ran for the hose.

"'Get Nelly out!' I cried to Steve; but after a second look, I called, 'No, don't you do it! Let her go! it's too late!'

"'I won't let her go!' he shouted; 'do you think I'll stand by and see Nelly burned to death!'

"'You'd be a fool to go in now! Look at that stable! Here! Stand back! Have you lost your wits?'

"'Let me go!' he cried; 'Jack, get out of the way!'

"But I threw him down and held him. I was bigger than he; older, and cooler-headed too.

"'There, I give in,' he said in a moment; 'it's wicked to lose time this way. Let me up, Jack, and we'll get the hose. I promise you I won't go in.'

"We ran for the hose, and turned on all the water we could command, and by this time mother and the servant girl had come from the house, and were helping us.

"We could hear Nelly struggling in her stall, and I tell you it made us sick! Unluckily we had chained her, in anticipation of her trying to get loose, and go after Prince. She'd never been left at home this way before, and we'd taken extra pains to secure her.

"The stable doors were fastened by a heavy bolt; again and again I tried to push it back, but it was so fiery hot I couldn't touch it, and when I tried to hammer it, the flames drove me off.

"There was nothing for it but to leave poor Nelly to her fate. It seemed as if she divined our intent, for, as we turned away, she uttered a piercing scream. Mother burst into tears.

"'I can't stand it,' she said, covering her ears.

"Again and again Nelly's voice rang out. Steve stood there, his face drawn and white. All at once he took out his watch.

"'It's twelve o'clock!' he cried; 'father'll be home in a moment, and if Prince hears Nelly he'll go mad. Head 'em off, Jack!'

"I didn't wait for another word, but ran with all my might down the road by which they always came.

"As fate would have it, they had chosen the other one that day, and were well along, before I caught sight of them. Father had taken Prince out of the plow, and harnessed him to a little single-seated gig we had. He was driving him, and Ned was walking behind. I saw Steve running toward them, but he was still at a distance.

"'Father,' I yelled at the top of my voice, 'stop! father! the stable's on fire. Turn Prince back. Nelly is burning!'

"Father didn't seem to understand, for although he listened, he kept driving slowly on.

"I shouted again, running toward them, and gesticulating frantically. All at once Ned caught my meaning, and bounding like a deer in front of the gig, grabbed Prince by the head to turn him, but at that very moment a terrible scream from poor Nelly split our ears, and in less time than it takes to tell there was a maddened horse plunging in midair, with four strong men clinging to him, trying to hold him back.

"'Let him go, boys! Let him go!' shouted father; 'it's no use! Let him go, I tell you! He'll kill us all!'

"'Oh, God! I can't let the old fellow burn up!' sobbed Steve.

"But Prince had begun to lay about him with his teeth, and father knocked Steve down to get him out of the way.

"I believe we all sobbed, as we watched the old hero go up that hill and into the stable; Nelly was quiet now, and the doors were down.

"We heard him groan once or twice, and then mother came to meet us, and took us all into the house.

"It's out yonder—the monument we put up. It's over both of them."

"Well, what has that horse story to do with men?" asked a sneering voice, when I had finished my little tale, and Mrs. Purblind and I were sitting silent.

I turned, and to my astonishment and disgust saw Mrs. Cynic, who had come in quietly, unobserved by me, as I was reading.

I should not have answered her a word, but Mrs. Purblind thought to avert an awkward situation, so she said:

"It illustrates the devotion of the masculine nature, I suppose."

"In horses? Yes; it's a pity that it hasn't been evoluted into men."

"It has," I answered curtly, "for those who are capable of seeing and appreciating it."

This probably made her angry, for she turned on me with her most evil expression:

"It's a mystery to me why, with your overweening admiration for the other sex, you haven't married, Miss Leigh. You must have had countless opportunities; child-like faith, such as yours, must be very attractive to them."

I stared at her a moment in silence; her insolence stupefied me. Then I think I opened the nearest window, and pitched her out. Mrs. Purblind insists I did not do that, exactly, but that I got rid of her. As she hasn't been in since, a desirable result was obtained, and I don't much care what the method may have been.

I aired my house the rest of the day, having a wish to cleanse it, and protect my moral nature, much as one would rid a place of sewer gas, to protect the physical being.

I was not in a very good temper after all this, and it annoyed me to see Randolph Chance coming in before taking his train. He had been calling oftener than usual of late, but he didn't seem to have much to say, and so his coming gave no especial pleasure.

To-day what talk we had ran on flowers for a time, when Mr. Chance, awkwardly and out-of-placedly, asked me how I liked the Reve d'or rose. This was the kind of rose I had received every morning, during my illness.

I looked at him inquiringly. I confess my heart was beating faster.

He flushed, and said abruptly:

"You must have known I sent you those."

"I did not," I answered rather coldly; "there was no card or note with them."

"I thought you'd know," he said with increasing embarrassment; and then he added, almost desperately, "you must know, Constance, that I love you."

"I know nothing," I replied, drawing myself up haughtily; "I take nothing of this kind for granted. If you want me to understand, you must come out openly."

"I have done enough, surely," he said, "enough to lead you to guess the truth."

"I guess nothing of this sort!" I reiterated; "what right have you to place me in this position? What right have you, or any other man to deprive a woman of one of her dearest privileges—that of being wooed?"

"Constance!" he cried, and all his embarrassment was gone, "aren't there a thousand ways of saying 'I love you?' and haven't I said it in every way but one?"

"That one was the most important of all," I answered; "I would have given more to hear those words than to receive every other token."

His face lighted up with a sudden flash, and he started impulsively toward me.

"Then you do love me, my darling—I have hardly dared to hope."

But I drew back, and answered passionately,

"No, I do not! I love no man who can trifle with a young girl, or any woman—no man who has the effrontery to expect some one to take for granted a courtship that has never existed!"

"For Heaven's sake, what do you mean?"

"Go to Miss Sprig and inquire; she has more reason to take your love for granted than I."

"I'll not go to her, but I shall leave you," he said, with a white face. "You certainly don't care for me, or you would never deal me such an unjust thrust as this."

And then I heard him close the front door. I think the neighborhood heard him.

I walked to the window. He was gone.

I told myself I was glad of it—that a good lesson had been taught.

Which of us was teacher remained somewhat obscure.

XII

It might reasonably be supposed that the event last narrated disturbed my life. It did in a measure, and for a time, but I was not very long in bringing it back to its accustomed channel.

Strange as it may seem, although we lived across the street from one another, I saw nothing of Mr. Chance for many weeks. Perhaps it is not strange though, after all, since each of us was taking pains to avoid the other, and we knew each other's habits of life pretty well by this time.

But if I didn't see him, I heard of him frequently enough, for Mrs. Purblind rarely ever met me without saying something about "Dolph," as she called him. She was exceedingly fond of him, and with good cause, for he was a most affectionate, thoughtful, unselfish brother. He was very different from her, and they were not confidential friends, when serious matters were concerned, but they were companionable, nevertheless.

It is not likely Mrs. Purblind realized that she was shut out from something that deeply concerned her brother; but she worried about him. She was certain he was ill—he had little appetite, and was in no way like himself, she said. Miss Sprig wondered what had come over him.

I believe Mrs. Purblind must have been deaf as well as blind, otherwise the neighborhood gossip regarding Mr. Chance and myself, which was rife a year ago, would certainly have reached her. Evidently she had heard nothing, and she continued to keep my innermost breast in a secret ferment, by pouring her fears and speculations into my ear. She even confided in me that she had for a long time suspected the existence of an affair between Miss Sprig and her brother, but this young woman declared that he never paid her the slightest attention of a matrimonial character; that he'd been very kind to her, very jolly, and friendly, but that was all.

I think that if Mount Vesuvius had leaped out of me, and taken its departure, I could scarce have felt more relieved. I really had been harboring a volcano for some time, and it was a hot tenant.

Shortly after hearing this latter piece of Mrs. Purblind's news, another bit was added.

"Dolph has gone away," she said, one day; "left suddenly, this morning. He confessed to being played out, and I'm sure he looks it. He's gone on to Buffalo, to brother Dave's."

That night I sat down and wrote a letter; when one has done wrong, his first conscious act should be to confess.

I was in a trying position; one is at such a time. Two months had elapsed, and Mr. Chance might have changed his mind and intent. Men do, occasionally; women, too. And indeed he never had asked me to marry him. True, that is the supposition when a man, with any real manhood about him, tells a woman he loves her—when he shows her marked attentions, in fact; but, as I said to Mr. Chance, I did not intend to take such things for granted. I had not changed in that respect. I had, however, become convinced that I was harsh and unjust to him. It is a blundering teacher who takes badness in a child for granted—does not wait for proof. It is an inspired teacher who ignores the bad sometimes, even after it has been proven. To think the worst, so some of the psychologists tell us, will often create the worst. Even a cook does well to make the most of her materials. Her dishes will be likely to turn out ill, if she treats the ingredients with disrespect. It would seem that I, who had in a manner made a specialty of matrimonial cookery, had something yet to learn. Randolph Chance had given me a lesson.

In my letter, I said that time and thought had shown me I had done him a wrong, and that I was very sorry; that, no doubt, he had changed in some feelings, and it was, perhaps, not likely we should meet very soon; but that I wished him to know I realized my mistake, and that I was still his friend.

The second day after I had written, I heard from him; our letters were penned the same night, and must have crossed each other. In his he said he had held off as long as he could, but was coming right back from Buffalo to see me.

He was certain he could explain everything; he had nothing to hide, and he hoped I would let him tell me what was in his heart; that for months he had known but one real wish, one real aspiration—to win me for his wife. He begged me to let him begin anew, and make an effort to attain this great end.

That evening, in the gloaming, I was at my study window. I could look into the parlor of the Thrush home. A shadow had fallen upon that dear nest; one of the little birdies had flown away, but it was now forever sheltered from all storms in the dear Christ's bosom, so all was well. The gentle little mother was nearly crushed at first, even more so than the father, though he felt the loss deeply; but erelong she lifted her sweet face, and smiled through her tears. And now, at the end of two weeks, she was to her husband, at least, as cheerful as ever, even more tender, and she made the home as bright as before. So many women are selfish in their grief, unwise too. They act as if their husbands were aliens, and did not share the sorrow. It is true the man usually recovers sooner than the woman from such a blow, but no one should blame him for that. His nature is different, necessarily different; not in kind, but in degree. It has to be; his is the outside battle; he must needs be rugged. But "a man's a man for a' that," and the woman who shuts him out in the hour of bereavement, or who darkens the home continuously, and overcasts its good cheer, is both selfish and foolish. In such cases husband and wife are parted, instead of being brought nearer to one another, as they should be when they have a little ambassador in the court of Heaven.

My heart was very tender that evening, and as I sat beside the glowing fire, before the lamps were lighted, my thoughts ran to Mrs. Purblind. The poor little woman had seemed sad of late, and I guessed, without word from her, that it was because her husband was going out so much at night. I did wish she could see some things as they really were.

She sat there with me that evening—in spirit, at least, on the opposite side of the fireplace, and her mournful face touched me deeply.

"He doesn't seem to care for his home," she said sadly.

"Make him care for it. Man is a domestic animal. If he doesn't stay at home, something is wrong."

"I do all I can," she answered in a dull tone.

"No doubt you do now," I said; "but learn more, and then you will improve."

"I was looking over some trunks in the attic to-day, and I came across my wedding gown. It called up so much! I can't get over it—" and she sobbed aloud.

I couldn't speak just then. The tears were too near.

"Oh, when first I wore that gown, how happy I was, and how I looked forward to the future! Everything was bright then, but now it's so changed that I'd hardly know it was the same—it isn't the same—I'm not the same, either——"

Here she broke down again.

I leaned over, and laid my hand on hers. You know she wasn't really there; the real Mrs. Purblind seldom talked over her affairs with me, but I could feel what she was suffering, none the less.

"I want to tell you something, if I may," I said.

She assented in a dumb sort of fashion, and I leaned a little nearer.

The firelight gleamed on the walls, and in its glow the pictures looked down kindly upon us. Soft shadows rested in the corners of the room, and an air of peace and comfort brooded throughout, as a bird upon her nest.

"Think a little while," I said gently; "think of his side. Is he quite the same as he was when he married?"

"Oh, no!" she exclaimed; "he was so loving and attentive then."

"Had he any hopes and plans? Enthusiasm? Did life look bright to him?"

A serious look traversed her face, as though she were entertaining a new thought.

"Look at him as he used to be," I continued.

And as I spoke, she saw that a young man with a fresh, sunny face—a healthy, happy, care-free face—was sitting in the ruddy firelight.

She gave a start.

"That is Joe as he used to be!" she said. "Oh, how he's changed!"

Even as she spoke, the young man faded away, and an older man—much older, apparently, careworn, and unhappy-looking—took his place.

The coals in the glowing grate sank, and the bright light suddenly died. A deep shadow rested upon the figure beside us; he was with us, and yet seemed so alone.

"Who would think a man could change that way in ten years!" exclaimed Mrs. Purblind; "would you believe it possible?"

"Not unless he had known many disappointments, and borne loads and cares beyond his years."

"I have never thought of that," she murmured, "I believe poor Joe has been disappointed too."

"He certainly has."

"It's too bad, and there's no help for it now," she added with a sob.

"Don't say that," I urged, laying my hand on hers again; "you close the gate of heaven when you say 'no hope.' There is always hope as long as there is a spark of life— any physician will tell you that. If you can be patient—be strong to bear, and wait—if you can make home bright, and not care, or not seem to care if he slights it and you, for weeks—months, maybe years—it takes so much longer to undo, than to do—there is every hope. He couldn't do this, but a woman—a real woman, is strong enough, with God on her side."

The dullness left her face, and an unselfish light dawned in its place. As she rose to go, she leaned over the other figure, and he looked up at her, with something of the old-time love.

I replenished the fire after they had gone—they went out together—and as I sat there thinking of it all, I heard a sudden rushing sound in the street.

I ran to the door, just in time to see a farm wagon, drawn by two strong horses, go pell-mell past my house, and overturn, as the frightened animals dashed around the corner. The neighborhood was agog in a moment, and I joined the rest in trying to help the occupants of the broken vehicle. We brought them into the house—the man and woman and a little child.

As soon as they were in the light, I knew them; they were some of my people—a German family, by the name of Abraham, who lived on a little farm just outside our suburb. They had been to me typical representatives of a stupid class, who have all the hardships of life, and none of its soft lights and shades. They were the kind that plant their pig-sty on the lake side of their house—put the pig-sty betwixt them and every other beauty, it seemed to me. What can life hold for such people? They know nothing of love, or any other joy. Merely an animal existence is theirs.

We fetched a doctor as speedily as possible—the parents were merely bruised, but the little child was badly hurt. At first we feared she was dying, and it was a relief to be told that she would probably live.

I went out of the room to get some bandages, and the doctor followed me. Returning suddenly, I ran upon an

uncxpected scene; up to that time, before us all, the parents
had seemed perfectly stolid; but just as I opened the door,
the wife and mother rose from her knees by the bed, and I
have seldom seen a look more expressive of tender love
than that with which her husband took her in his arms.

We have many things to learn in the next world; one of
these, I am sure, will be, not to judge by the life upon the
surface. There is a deep fount of feeling beneath, and often
it is those whom we least suspect, who dip down into it.

I was still busy with these people, when Randolph Chance
walked in upon me. His kind heart needed no prompting to
join in our little attentions, and he was of especial use in
getting a vehicle to take the family home.

After they had gone, and we found ourselves alone, a great
embarrassment seemed to seize him in a fatal grasp.

By and by I realized that I was really getting incensed, and
I was afraid I should soon be in the position of the man
who went to another, whom he had ill-treated, to apologize
for his bad conduct, and, "By Jove, sir"—to use his own
phrase, "I hit him again."

I tried to keep my letter before my eyes. I didn't want to be
forced by that inexorable tyrant—conscience—to write
another. And I should, if I didn't hold on to myself, and this
man didn't behave differently.

To avoid a clash, I set to work to clear away some of the
confusion consequent upon the accident, and he helped me
in this.

One would suppose that might serve to cool him, and it did indeed, to such an extent that, upon our settling down again, he began the most commonplace conversation, giving me some incidents of his trip; discussing the scenery; weather; population, and general aspects of Buffalo; with much more of the dryest, most disagreeable stuff, that a man ever had the temerity to use, as a means of wasting a woman's evening.

To employ a childish phrase—it best fits the occasion—I grew madder and madder, until at last matters within me rose to such a height, that when he began to tell of his brother's house in Buffalo, and to dwell upon the peculiarities of its furniture, I felt peculiar enough to hurl all of mine at him.

The number of things I thought of that evening would form a library of energetic literature. Among other resolves, I determined from that day on, if I lived till my hair whitened—lived till I raised my third or fourth crop of teeth, never, never, to give Randolph Chance another thought. There was one comfort: he did not know, nor did any one else, what a complete goose I had made of myself; but, though I had been most foolish, thanks to a sober, Puritanic ancestry, I still had myself in hand; my hysterics had been occasional and secluded, and I was not wholly gone daft. I could recover; I would! and then, if ever he came to my feet, he would learn that some things don't rise, after once they are cold.

I was calm enough when he at last decided to go, and instead of running on excitedly, as I had been vaguely conscious of doing part of the evening, I really conversed. Indeed, to speak modestly, I think I was rather interesting. I

had forgotten what he had called for. So had he—
apparently.

All I hoped was that he did not intend to bore me with
frequent repetitions of this call. I had better use for my
evenings than such waste of time as chatting with him. I
cast about me for some suitable excuse to shut off future
inflictions, and at last hit upon one that I thought might
answer.

"I suppose I must sacrifice myself for a while," I said
cheerfully; "I have had a deal of business swoop down
upon me, and in order to dispatch it, must shut myself up
for a time, and forego the joys of society."

Instantly his old embarrassment came back upon him, as a
small boy's enemy—supposed to be vanquished—darts
around the corner, and renews the attack.

He started to go; came back; returned to the door; again
came back; colored vividly—looked at me imploringly.
And as I looked at him my anger, my coldness—all
vanished, and I exclaimed:

"Randolph Chance, why don't you say it!"

"Some things are awfully hard to say. I can write—— Oh
Constance! you might have mercy on me!"

"Well," I said, laughing—I could almost see the light upon
my face—"I suppose you want me to marry you."

"You can't get away now!" he cried, a second later.

The walls heard a much-smothered voice—

"I don't want to."

Now this little scene, I suppose, is what makes Randolph always say I proposed to him. This remark, oft repeated, sometimes under very trying circumstances, is his one disagreeableness. But I let it pass without comment, for I realize it is the spout to the kettle, and I am thankful that the steam has so safe and harmless an outlet. If I were to boil him too hard, he would probably overflow, and dim the fire; but I am very cautious, and love still burns with a clear, bright flame.